Dirty Bertie

TOTALLY EPIC

DAVID ROBERTS WRITTEN BY **ALAN MACDONALD**

Dirty Bertie

Collect all the
Dirty Bertie books!

Contents

STRIPES PUBLISHING LIMITED
An imprint of the Little Tiger Group
1 Coda Studios, 189 Munster Road,
London SW6 6AW

A paperback original
First published in Great Britain in 2020

Characters created by David Roberts
Text copyright © Alan MacDonald
Burp! 2007 · *Monster!* 2016 · *Disco!* 2017
Illustrations copyright © David Roberts
Burp! 2007 · *Monster!* 2016 · *Disco!* 2017

ISBN: 978-1-78895-198-2

MIX
Paper from
responsible sources
FSC® C020471

The Forest Stewardship Council® (FSC®) is a global, not-for-profit organization dedicated to the promotion of responsible forest management worldwide. FSC® defines standards based on agreed principles for responsible forest stewardship that are supported by environmental, social, and economic stakeholders. To learn more, visit www.fsc.org

10 9 8 7 6 5 4 3 2 1

Dirty Bertie

BURP!

For Henry, who seems to have picked
up some of Bertie's dirty habits
(apologies to the hamster) ~ D R

Contents

CHAPTER 1

Bertie was the only one in his class who actually liked school dinners. Lumpy mash with gloopy gravy. Wormy spaghetti with meatballs. Cold custard with slimy skin on top. Bertie loved them all.

"Ugh! I don't know how you can eat it!" said Darren at lunch on Friday. Bertie slurped his rice pudding and gave an extremely satisfied burp.

"Aren't you going to finish yours?"

"No," said Darren. "It looks like frogspawn."

"Pass it over," said Bertie.

Just then Miss Skinner, the Head, swept into the dining hall with a woman in a white coat. Miss Skinner rapped on a table to get their attention. "I want you all to meet Miss Beansprout, who is our new Head Dinner Lady," she said. "Miss Beansprout has lots of splendid ideas to improve our school meals."

Dirty Bertie

Miss Beansprout gazed at them fondly. "Children," she said, "it's my job to make sure you all have a healthy, wholesome diet. Who can tell me something that is healthy and delicious?"

Pamela raised her hand. "An orange," she said.

"Very good," beamed Miss Beansprout.

"An avocado," said Know-All Nick, showing off.

"Excellent," said Miss Beansprout.

"Nuts," said Bertie.

Dirty Bertie

"Wonderful. Nuts are very good for you," nodded Miss Beansprout.

"Great," said Bertie. "Will we be having doughnuts tomorrow?"

"Stop talking and get on with your dinner," snapped Miss Beansprout.

On Monday Mrs Mould wasn't serving dinners behind the hatch as usual. In her place was Miss Beansprout. She had written a menu on the board.

🍎 Today's Menu
Cabbage and chickpea Soup
Broccoli Bake with Beetroot Salad
Carrot cake Surprise
Low-Fat Yoghurt
apple or banana (for a treat)

Dirty Bertie

Bertie and his friends stared in horror. Surely this was some kind of joke? *Broccoli? Cabbage?* Was she trying to KILL them?

"What's this?" asked Bertie.

"Lots of lovely fruit and vegetables," said Miss Beansprout. "Just what growing children need."

"But where are the chips?" asked Bertie.

"No greasy chips," said Miss Beansprout.

"Where is the custard?"

"No horrible custard."

"Where's the jam roly-poly pudding?"

"No stodgy puddings full of nasty sugar," said Miss Beansprout. "From now on we're all going to be eating delicious greens and nourishing salads."

"I love salad," said Know-All Nick. "A big helping for me!"

Dirty Bertie

Bertie gave him a withering look.

"Cabbage Soup or Broccoli Bake?"
Miss Beansprout asked him.

"Can't I just have pudding?" asked
Bertie.

"Broccoli Bake it is," said Miss
Beansprout. She ladled a gloopy green
mess on to Bertie's plate. SPLAT!

Next to it went the salad, swimming in beetroot juice.

"Yoghurt or Carrot Cake Surprise?" asked Miss Beansprout.

"What's the surprise?" asked Bertie hopefully.

"The carrots are organic. That means they're bursting with vitamins!" beamed Miss Beansprout.

Bertie carried his tray over to a table to sit down. "I can't eat this," he grumbled, staring at his plate.

"You haven't tasted it yet," said Know-All Nick.

"Quite right, Nicholas," said Miss Skinner, who was on dinner duty. "Perhaps some *fussy* children could learn from your example. Eat up, Bertie, it looks delicious!"

Dirty Bertie

Bertie raised a forkful of green gloop to his lips. Darren leaned over to whisper in his ear.

"Boiled bogeys with squashed slug salad."

Bertie set down his fork. Suddenly he didn't feel at all hungry.

CHAPTER 2

Miss Beansprout's dinners got worse.
On Tuesday they had Celery and Nut
Crumble. On Wednesday it was Liver
Casserole and Sprouts followed by
Stewed Prunes. Bertie couldn't take any
more. At break time he called an
emergency meeting in the playground.

"If I eat one more vegetable I'm going

to be sick," he groaned.

"So am I," said Eugene.

"I couldn't stop burping yesterday," said Darren. "Great big smelly burps!"

"I know, I was sitting next to you," moaned Donna.

"Well it's no good just grumbling, we've got to do something," said Bertie.

"We could kidnap Miss Beansprout and lock her in a dungeon," suggested Darren.

"Good idea," said Donna. "Except we haven't got a dungeon."

"Well I'm not putting up with it any longer," said Bertie. "They can't make us eat it."

"Can't they?" asked Eugene.

"No," said Bertie. "Not if we all refuse. Not if we all say we're going on strike."

Dirty Bertie

Eugene looked anxious. "Won't we get into trouble?"

"Listen," said Bertie. "We're not eating anything until they give us back our old dinners. Right?"

"Right," agreed the others. Even lumpy mash and gloopy gravy would be better than the sickly slop Miss Beansprout gave them.

At lunchtime Bertie joined the dinner queue.

"What would you like? Liver Casserole and Sprouts?" asked Miss Beansprout.

"No, thank you," said Bertie.

"A big slice of Spinach Pie?"

"No thanks," said Bertie. "I don't want anything."

"Nothing? Don't be silly. You have to eat," said Miss Beansprout.

Bertie shook his head firmly. "I'd rather go without."

"So would I," said Darren.

"And me," said Donna. She nudged Eugene.

"Oh, me too … please," said Eugene.

Dirty Bertie

Miss Beansprout sent for Miss Skinner. "These children are refusing to eat their dinner," she said.

"Which children?" said Miss Skinner. The others all looked at Bertie.

"We're on strike," Bertie informed her. "Till you bring back the old dinners."

Miss Skinner smiled a thin smile. "I see. You don't want any dinner? Well that's fine with me."

"Pardon?" said Bertie.

"It's fine. Go without," said Miss Skinner. "Off you go!"

Bertie and his friends trooped away with empty plates. They sat down at a table and watched the other children chewing and slurping their food.

"I'm hungry," moaned Darren.

"So am I," groaned Eugene.

"I'm starving! I could even eat a carrot," said Donna.

Eugene gazed over at Know-All Nick's plate. "Couldn't we just have pudding?"

"NO!" said Bertie. "We're on strike, remember? We're not eating until they give us back our old dinners."

"But I haven't had anything since breakfast," grumbled Darren. "If I don't eat soon I'll starve to death!"

"Huh!" said Bertie. "Well it would just serve them right if we did. Maybe it'd teach them a lesson."

CHAPTER 3

SLAM! Bertie arrived home from school.
His mum was in the kitchen talking on
the phone.

"Yes," she said. "Don't worry, I'll speak
to him. He's just come in now."

Bertie had the feeling it was time to
make a swift exit. He ran upstairs.

"BERTIE!" yelled his mum. "Down here

now. I want a word with you."

Bertie shuffled into the kitchen.

"What's all this about not eating your school dinners?" demanded Mum.

"Oh," said Bertie. "That."

"Yes, that. I just had Miss Skinner on the phone and she sounds very cross."

"It's not my fault," said Bertie. "The dinners are horrible! They're full of vegetables."

"Vegetables are good for you."

"But Mum, they're making us eat broccoli. And beetroot! And carrots!"

"Good," said Mum. "It sounds very healthy."

"How can it be healthy when I feel ill just looking at it?" asked Bertie.

"Don't make such a fuss, Bertie. It's only a few carrots!"

Dirty Bertie

"But Mum…"

"No buts," said Mum. "Tomorrow you eat all your dinner."

Bertie sighed. "OK."

"Promise me," said Mum.

"I promise," said Bertie.

As he went upstairs he smiled to himself. He'd promised to eat his dinner – but he hadn't said what would be in it, had he?

Dirty Bertie

PEEP! Miss Skinner blew her whistle for the start of school. Bertie hurriedly stuffed something down his jumper and fell into line.

"What if she catches you?" hissed Darren.

"She won't," replied Bertie.

"No talking at the back!" yelled Miss Skinner. "In you go."

The line of children began to file past the Head, who watched them with narrowed eyes. Bertie kept his head down. Another few metres and he was home and dry. An arm shot out and barred his way. Uh oh.

"Bertie," said Miss Skinner.

"Yes, Miss?"

Dirty Bertie

"What's that lump under your jumper?"

"Lump, Miss? Nothing, Miss."

"Really?" Miss Skinner's finger prodded his jumper. It crackled and rustled.

"Hands up," ordered the Head Teacher.

"What?" said Bertie.

"You heard me, hands in the air."

Bertie raised both his hands. A bag of crisps fell out of his jumper. Then two more.

"Pockets," said Miss Skinner.

Bertie turned out his pockets. Some sweets and chocolate bars scattered at Miss Skinner's feet.

"You know the rules, Bertie," she said. "No crisps or sweets in school." The chocolate disappeared into her pocket.

Dirty Bertie

Later that day, Bertie passed the staff room on his way to lunch. He heard raised voices inside. "Thank goodness we don't have to survive on school dinners," said Miss Boot.

"Yes, they really are unpleasant," replied Miss Skinner. "Have another piece."

Bertie opened the door a crack and peeped in.

Dirty Bertie

He could see his teachers eating something. It was a bar of chocolate. *His* bar of chocolate. Bertie gasped. Well this time they'd gone too far. Nobody stole Bertie's chocolate and got away with it.

In the dining room Bertie stared. All his friends were eating their dinner.

"I thought we were on strike," Bertie scowled.

"Sorry, Bertie. I've got to eat. My mum made me promise," replied Eugene.

"Mine too," said Darren.

"Never mind, at least we tried," sighed Donna.

Bertie didn't answer. He wasn't beaten yet. If only he could think of some way to get revenge. He stared at the sloppy cauliflower cheese on Eugene's plate…

"It looks disgusting," he said.

"Yeah," agreed Darren. "Like flies in custard."

"Worms in ice cream," said Donna.

"Maggot jelly," said Eugene.

Bertie's mouth fell open. Why hadn't he thought of it before? Miss Beansprout was always boasting that her meals were made with fresh ingredients… Well maybe he would add a few fresh ingredients of his own!

CHAPTER 4

Next day Bertie waited impatiently for break time.

BRIIING! The bell sounded and the class thundered out into the playground. Bertie doubled back and slipped across the dining hall to the kitchen. He pushed open the door to check the coast was clear. Miss Beansprout was humming to

Dirty Bertie

herself at the sink in the back room. He would have to move fast. Bertie tiptoed over to the fridge and opened the door.

There on the top shelf was his target – a large bowl full of green salad. Bertie pulled out the tin he'd borrowed from his dad's fishing bag and took off the lid. Inside was a sea of fat wriggling grubs.

"Dinner time, boys!" he whispered.

Half an hour later, Miss Skinner sat down to eat her lunch. She raised a forkful of green salad to her mouth and began to chew. Strange, she thought, today it tasted rather odd – sort of salty and squishy. She gazed down at her plate.

Dirty Bertie

Something in the salad moved. It raised its head and wiggled around.

"ARGHHHHH!" screamed Miss Skinner. "MAGGOTS!"

Her plate smashed on the floor. She clutched at her throat. Maggots! And she had just swallowed a whole mouthful! She grabbed a jug of water and glugged it down.

"Miss Beansprout!" she screeched. The Head Dinner Lady came running.

Everywhere she looked children were yelling, screaming and spitting their food on the floor. What on earth was going on?

"Look!" thundered Miss Skinner pointing at her plate. "Look!"

"I … I don't understand," stammered Miss Beansprout. "The salad was fresh this morning."

"Fresh?" thundered Miss Skinner. "It's crawling with maggots! Are you trying to poison me?"

Dirty Bertie

"I'm sorry, Miss Skinner. It won't happen again."

"You're right, Miss Beansprout," fumed the Head. "It certainly won't."

The following Monday Bertie was back in the lunch queue once again. The board with today's healthy menu had vanished. There was no sign of Miss Beansprout. Mrs Mould was back behind the hatch in her grubby apron. Bertie couldn't wait. *No more yucky beetroot or boring broccoli,* he thought. *Mash and gravy, here I come!*

Mrs Mould slopped a pile of spaghetti on to his plate. Bertie stared. It was sticky, wriggling and wiggling.

Just like…

Dirty Bertie

He clapped a hand over his mouth
and fled from the dining room.

"What's wrong with him?" asked
Eugene.

"Dunno," shrugged Darren. "I thought
he liked wormy spaghetti."

CHAPTER 1

Bertie was busy working on an experiment in his bedroom. For weeks now he had been collecting the ingredients to make a stink bomb.

Bertie's Super-smelly STINKBOMB - Mark ①

1 lump of pongy cheese   1 sweaty football sock
4 rotten eggs   3 mouldy cabbage leaves
1 tin of dog food   Dog hairs - a good handful

Dirty Bertie

Slip! Slop! Bertie gave the ingredients a good stir with a pencil and sniffed the murky brown goo. *Not bad*, he thought.

It just needed a few more days to get really good and pongy. Bertie couldn't wait to try out his stink bomb at school. Maybe he could smuggle it into Miss Boot's desk? Or, better still, splat Know-All Nick on the way home from school. Whiffer padded over and poked his nose into the plastic pot.

"Uh uh. No, Whiffer," said Bertie. "It's not for eating."

Someone was coming. Bertie quickly slammed the lid on the pot and hid it in his bedside cupboard.

Dirty Bertie

Mum poked her head around the door. "Bertie, what are you doing?" she asked suspiciously.

"Nothing," said Bertie. "Just playing."

Mum sniffed the air. "What's that funny smell?"

"Smell? I can't smell anything."

"It's disgusting," said Mum. "It smells like a family of skunks!"

"Does it?" Bertie looked pleased. The stink bomb must be a real humdinger if you could smell it from inside a cupboard. Mum was sniffing round the room trying to detect where the nasty smell was coming from. Bertie knew he'd have to act quickly before she investigated the bedside cupboard.

"PHEW, WHIFFER! Was that you?" he said, holding his nose.

Whiffer wagged his tail.

"That dog," sighed Mum. She turned back to Bertie. "I thought I asked you to tidy your room."

"It *is* tidy," replied Bertie.

Mum gave him a withering look. "Bertie! There's rubbish everywhere!"

Bertie inspected his room. Everything was where it normally was. On the floor.

"I like it like this," he explained.

"Well, I don't and I need you to tidy it up," said Mum. "Suzy's having a friend for a sleepover tonight."

"Who?" asked Bertie.

Suzy appeared in the doorway. "Bella," she said.

Bertie groaned. Not Bossy Bella. Of all Suzy's friends she was the worst. She would be trying to boss him around all night.

"And they'll be sleeping in here," said Mum.

Bertie's mouth fell open. He felt sick, he felt dizzy. "HERE? In MY ROOM?" he said.

"Yes," said Mum. "Your room's much bigger than Suzy's. We can put up the Z bed."

"But … but where am I going to sleep?"

"In Suzy's room."

Dirty Bertie

"NO!" yelled Bertie.
"NO!" screamed Suzy.
"It's only for one night," said Mum.
"I can't sleep in here. I'll catch fleas!" grumbled Suzy.

"Nonsense. Bertie's going to tidy up."

"Tidy up? It needs disinfecting!" said Suzy. "And what's that horrible smell?"

Mum pointed at Whiffer. "He needs to go back to the vet's."

CHAPTER 2

DING DONG! Bertie could hear voices downstairs. Bossy Bella had arrived.

"Hello, Bella!" said Mum brightly.

"Hello," replied Bella.

"Have a super time, pumpkin!" said Bella's mum, kissing her on the cheek. "I'll pick you up in the morning."

Mum shut the door.

"Well then, why don't you show Bella where she's sleeping, Suzy?"

Bella handed Suzy her suitcase and clumped upstairs after her.

They found Bertie on his bed reading a comic.

"Get out," said Suzy.

"You get out," said Bertie. "This is my room."

"Not tonight. Mum says we've got to sleep in here, remember?"

Bella scowled. She hated little brothers. If she had a little brother she would give him to a charity shop.

"I'm not sleeping in his bed," she pointed. "It smells."

"You're the one that smells," replied Bertie.

"You do."

"No, you do."

"No, you do."

"Ignore him," said Suzy. "Let's play princesses. You can be Princess Bella."

"Princess Smella, you mean," sniggered Bertie.

Bella yanked Bertie off the bed. She twisted his arm.

"OW!" cried Bertie. He gave her a shove. Bella stumbled and fell on to the Z bed. TWANG! It collapsed.

"Waaaahhhh!" she howled.

Mum came running upstairs. "What's going on?" she demanded.

"Bertie hit me," whined Bella.

"Bertie!" said Mum crossly.

"I didn't!" said Bertie. "She practically broke my arm!"

"It was him that started it," said Suzy. "He's spoiling our game."

"Bertie, go to your room!" ordered Mum.

"This is my room," said Bertie.

"I mean go to Suzy's room and stay there till supper."

Bertie stormed out. It wasn't fair. He'd get those sneaky girls for this.

Dirty Bertie

"Supper time!" called Mum.

Bertie bounded downstairs. He was
starving. He'd been in Suzy's room for
hours and there was nothing to play with.
Not even a pirate cutlass or water pistol.
In the kitchen he could smell pizza and
chips.

"Yum," said Bertie, helping himself to a
large slice of pizza.

"Manners, Bertie!" said Mum.

"Yes, Bertie," said Suzy. "We always
serve guests first."

Bertie reluctantly put the pizza back
and pushed the plate under Bella's nose.
Bella pulled a face. "I don't like pizza."

"Oh dear, never mind, have some
salad," said Mum.

Dirty Bertie

"I don't like salad," grumbled Bella.

"Then just eat the chips," sighed Mum, piling some on Bella's plate.

"I don't like these chips. They're not like my mum's," complained Bella.

"Great, all the more for me!" said Bertie, reaching over to grab Bella's plate.

"Bertie!" snapped Dad.

Bella grabbed her plate and held on. Bertie pulled. Bella pulled back. The chips

catapulted into the air and landed on the floor.

Bertie bent down. He picked up a chip, wiped it on his shirt and ate it.

"BERTIE!" yelled Mum.

"What did I do now?" asked Bertie with his mouth full.

"Get down from the table and go to your room!" ordered Mum.

Bella looked at Suzy. They both smiled.

CHAPTER 3

After supper the girls sat down to watch TV. Bertie burst in and threw himself into an armchair. "Where's the remote? *Alien Arthur* is on!" he said.

"We're watching the other side," said Suzy. "It's *Make Me a Pop Princess*."

"What?" gasped Bertie. "But I always watch *Alien Arthur* on Saturdays."

Dirty Bertie

"Let's take a vote," said Suzy. "Who wants Bertie's programme?"

Bertie put up his hand.

"Who wants to watch *Pop Princess*?" Suzy and Bella both raised their hands.

"Two votes to one, you lose," sneered Bella.

Bertie slumped in his chair miserably. This was turning out to be the worst Saturday ever. And it was all the fault of Suzy and her bossy friend. He couldn't even go up to his room to work on his stink bomb because Mum said he had to keep out. Well, he wasn't going to be beaten that easily. There was no way he was sleeping in Suzy's bedroom tonight. Her walls were covered in posters of ponies and drippy pop stars. It was enough to give anyone nightmares!

Dirty Bertie

Nightmares – that wasn't such a bad idea. Bertie slipped out of the room. A cunning plan had started to form in his head.

THUMP, THUMP, THUMP! Bertie was banging on the bathroom door.

Bella opened up.

"What?"

"I need the toilet. You've been in there hours!" complained Bertie.

Bella came out of the bathroom and barged past him.

"Goodnight, Bella!" said Bertie sweetly.

"Huh," she grunted.

Dirty Bertie

"I hope you can sleep," said Bertie.

Bella stopped. She turned round. "Why shouldn't I sleep?"

"You mean Suzy didn't tell you?"

"Tell me what?" said Bella.

Bertie lowered his voice.

"That my room's haunted."

"Ha ha, very funny," said Bella.

"Why do you think I've been begging to sleep in Suzy's room?" said Bertie.

"You didn't beg, your mum made you."

Bertie shook his head. He glanced around. "It's the noises," he whispered. "They keep me awake."

"Noises?" said Bella.

"The bumps and thumps. The moans and groans," said Bertie.

"Oh," said Bella, turning rather pale.

"Still, some people don't hear them.
It's only if you're scared of ghosts. You're
not, are you?"

"Me?" said Bella. "Course not."

"That's OK then. Sweet dreams!"

Bertie closed his door and smiled to
himself. *That ought to do it*, he thought.

Eleven o'clock. Bella was tossing and
turning in her bed. She couldn't sleep.

Her mattress was too lumpy. The room was too dark. Worst of all, she kept imagining she heard strange noises. Of course Bertie had been making it up. Suzy said he was. There was no such thing as ghosts.

CREAK, CREAK, CREAK!

What was that? Bella held her breath.

THUMP, THUMP, THUMP!

It sounded like footsteps on the landing. Bella gripped the covers tightly.

"Suzy?" she hissed. "Suzy. Are you awake?"

There was no answer from the Z bed.

RATTLE, RATTLE! went the door handle.

"EEEEEEEEEHHH!" went the door as it swung open by itself.

"Help!" whimpered Bella, diving under the covers. "Who's there?"

Dirty Bertie

She peeped out. There it was! A ghost
stumbling through the dark towards her.

"Wooooooooh!" it moaned.
"Wooooooooh!"

"Suzy," croaked Bella. "Suzy, wake up!"

"Wooooooooooh," moaned the ghost.

Closer and closer it came. Bella could

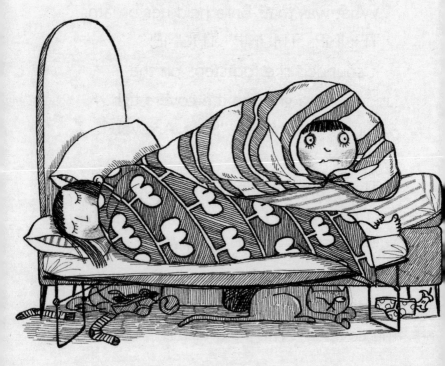

see its bare white feet.

"You must leave this place!" it moaned. "Leave this … OUCH!"

A pillow had thwacked the ghost on the back of the head. Suzy yanked off the ghost's white sheet, revealing its blue pyjamas.

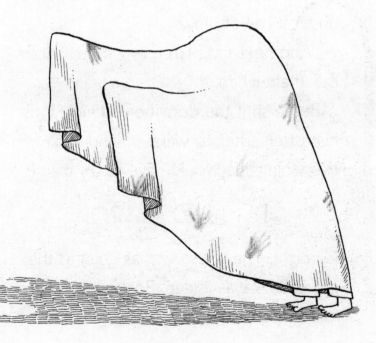

Dirty Bertie

"BERTIE!" snarled Suzy.

"Um, hello," said Bertie.

"Get out," said Suzy. "Get out and don't come back."

"Or what?" said Bertie.

WHUMP! A pillow whacked Bertie in the face. THUMP! Another clouted him on the ear. Bertie fled from the room under a hail of blows.

"And next time I'm telling Mum!" Suzy called after him.

Bertie shut the door behind him. Trust his rotten sister to wake up and spoil everything. He would have to try plan B.

Midnight. The house was as quiet as the grave. Suzy was asleep. Bossy Bella was asleep. Bertie was not asleep. He was creeping along the landing with something in his hand. He opened his bedroom door and stole inside. Now where to hide? His eyes fell on the windowsill above Bella's bed. Perfect!

Bella was talking in her sleep. "Get off. It's my go," she mumbled.

Bertie peeped out from behind the curtains. He brought out a big plastic spider on a string. Slowly he began to lower the spider towards his victim. Lower and lower it dangled, spinning round on its string. Bertie leaned out a little further to get a better view. The spider brushed Bella's hair. Bella's eyes snapped open. They bulged with fear. A giant black tarantula was inches from her face. Its red eyes were staring at her. It waggled its eight hairy legs.

Dirty Bertie

"ARGGHHHHHHHH!" screamed Bella.

Bertie was so startled he slipped off the windowsill and landed on top of Bella, who kicked and screamed.

"ARGH! GEROFFME! HEEEELP!"

The noise woke up Suzy.

"Muuuuuuum! Bertie's in our room!"

CLICK! The bedroom light came on. Mum stood in the doorway wrapped in her dressing gown.

"Bertie!" she seethed. "What do you think you're doing?"

"There was a huge black spider!" wailed Bella. "It was in my hair!"

Mum bent down. She picked the plastic spider off the floor and dangled it under Bertie's nose.

"Yours, I think," she said.

"Oh, um, thanks. I was looking for

that," said Bertie.

Mum glared at him. "Go to your room.
And if I catch you out of bed one more
time there'll be no sweets for a month."

Bertie trooped back to his room. He
closed the door behind him and got into
bed. Operation Ghost had failed. So had
Operation Spider. He thought he better
not try Operation Ants in the Pants. It
looked like he'd be sleeping in Suzy's
bed tonight after all.

CHAPTER 4

Meanwhile, in Bertie's bedroom, Bella was still awake. She wished Suzy's mum hadn't mentioned sweets. Thinking of sweets always made her hungry. She'd practically had nothing at all for supper.

At home she always kept a stash of sweets handy in case she got hungry at bedtime. Maybe Suzy's horrible little brother had some hidden somewhere?

Bella looked under the bed. Nothing there. She looked under the pillow. Nothing. She opened the bedside cupboard. On the shelf was a small plastic pot. Eagerly, Bella took it out and read the words scrawled on the side.

Ahaa! Sweeties! thought Bella.

She prised off the lid and peered inside.

A foul, putrid smell hit her like a force-ten gale. The pong of mouldy cabbage and rotten eggs filled the room. Bella clapped a hand to her mouth. She was going to be sick. She couldn't breathe.

"AHHHH! UGGGHHHHH!" she cried, dropping the stink bomb.

Suzy woke up.

Dirty Bertie

"Bella! What are you ... EURGH! What's that dreadful stink?" she gasped.

"I'm dying!" choked Bella. "I'm suffocating! Let me out!"

BANG! BANG! BANG!

Someone was hammering on Bertie's door.

Suzy and Bella burst in. "I need my bedroom back!" panted Suzy.

"What?" asked Bertie.

"It's horrible! It stinks! You've got to let us sleep in here!" begged Suzy.

"What are you talking about?"

"The smell – from that thing! It's choking us."

It dawned on Bertie – the stink bomb. He'd forgotten all about it.

"So you want me to give you back your bedroom?" he said slowly.

"Yes, yes. Please, Bertie! We can't sleep in there!" said Suzy.

"Hmmm," said Bertie. "I'll have to think about it."

"We'll do anything!" pleaded Bella.

Bertie raised his eyebrows. "Anything?"

Five minutes later Bertie was settled back in his own bed. True the room was a little whiffy, but he didn't really mind. Once you got used to it, the smell wasn't so bad – he couldn't see why the

Dirty Bertie

girls were making such a fuss. In any case all that mattered was he was back in his own room. And tomorrow Suzy and Bella had promised to play whatever he wanted. Bertie had already thought of a good game – it was called Pass the Stink Bomb.

CHAPTER 1

"Dog training classes?" Bertie stared at his mum in horror.

"Yes. No arguments, please, Bertie," said Mum.

"But why do I have to go?"

"Because someone has to take Whiffer. He can't go on his own."

"Why can't you take him?" asked Bertie.

"I'm far too busy."

"What about Dad then?"

"Oh no," said Dad hastily. "I'm *really* busy. Anyway he's your dog."

"But he doesn't need training!" protested Bertie.

Mum snorted. "Bertie! He barks every time the doorbell goes."

"And he's always climbing on the sofa," grumbled Dad.

"He licks food off your plate," said Mum. "And last week he did a poo on Mrs Nicely's lawn."

"He's a dog," said Bertie. "That's what dogs do!"

"Well it's high time he learned to behave," said Mum firmly. "And I'm told this dog trainer can work wonders."

Bertie sighed. It wasn't fair. He didn't

want to take Whiffer to training classes.
He got quite enough classes at school.

"Anyway, he *is* trained," he argued. "I've
been training him for ages."

"Bertie, he does what he likes," said
Mum.

"Not always," said Bertie. "Sometimes
he listens to me."

Mum gave him one of her looks.
Whiffer was dozing on his cushion in the
corner. Bertie turned to him and
pointed.

"Stay, Whiffer," he ordered. "STAY!"

Whiffer opened one eye lazily then went on dozing.

"See?" said Bertie. "Like I said – he does what I say."

Mum folded her arms. "Very funny. You are taking him to classes and that is the end of it."

The following Friday evening Dad drove Bertie and Whiffer to the leisure centre.

In the big hall dogs of all shapes and sizes waited with their owners. Whiffer pulled at his lead and whined. He wanted to make friends.

The trainer was called Miss Bowser. She had wiry hair and a face like a bad-tempered bulldog. Bertie could see why animals would obey her.

Dirty Bertie

Miss Bowser clapped her hands and told everyone to line up for inspection.

"Mmm," she said, patting a red setter. "Good, good. Splendid."

When she came to Whiffer she stopped and clicked her tongue.

"And what have we here?"

"My dog," said Bertie.

"I can see it's a dog. I mean what is his *name*?"

"He's called Whiffer."

"Whiffer?" she barked. "That's an odd name for a dog."

"Well he can be pretty smelly, especially when you're watching TV," explained Bertie. "Sometimes he does one and the pong's so bad you can smell it upstairs."

"Good gracious!" said Miss Bowser, drawing back a little.

Dirty Bertie

"I don't think he can help it," said Bertie.

"He will LEARN to help it," Miss Bowser replied grimly. "In my classes dogs do what they are told." She eyed Whiffer and raised a stern finger.

"SIT!" she ordered.

Whiffer sat. Bertie was amazed. He'd never done that for anyone before.

CHAPTER 2

The class began. Miss Bowser handed out dog biscuits.

"Treats must be earned," she told her class. "A naughty dog does not get a treat. Let's begin with a simple command. Teaching your dog to come when called."

Bertie groaned. He'd tried a million times

to get Whiffer to come. The only time he came was when his dog bowl was full.

"Step away from your dog and turn to face them," instructed Miss Bowser.

Bertie walked away from Whiffer. When he turned round, Whiffer was right behind him, wagging his tail. He could smell dog biscuits.

"No, Whiffer. You stay over there," said Bertie. "You come when I say 'Come', OK?"

Whiffer licked his hand and tried to nose in Bertie's pockets. Bertie dragged him back to his place by the collar.

"Now call your dog by name," said Miss Bowser. "When he comes give him a treat. And remember, heaps and heaps of praise."

"Whiffer! Come, boy!" called Bertie.

Dirty Bertie

Whiffer looked the other way.

"Come, boy. Come! COME!" yelled Bertie.

Whiffer was the only dog in the hall who hadn't moved. The other owners cooed and fussed over their dogs, who were wolfing down their biscuits. Miss Bowser strode over to Bertie.

"Where is your treat?" she boomed.

"Um, in my pocket."

"No, no, you have to let him see it! Give it to me!"

Miss Bowser held out her hand with the dog biscuit. Whiffer barked and flew at her – a whirlwind of fur and legs and tongue.

Miss Bowser found herself pinned to the floor, with Whiffer on top of her, crunching his biscuit happily.

Dirty Bertie

"How did it go?" asked Mum when Bertie got home later that evening.

"It was terrible," groaned Bertie, slumping into a chair. "It's worse than school."

Whiffer padded over to his cushion and flopped down wearily.

"Never mind," said Mum. "It's only the first lesson. I'm sure it will get better."

"You haven't met Miss Bowser," said Bertie darkly. "She shouts all the time – even when she's standing right next to you. I bet she used to be in the army. I bet she got tired of shouting at soldiers all day and decided she'd get a job shouting at dogs and their owners."

"As long as Whiffer does what he's told I don't mind," said Mum.

Dirty Bertie

"That's just it, he doesn't!" moaned Bertie. "He gets mixed up. He sits when he's meant to come and when I say 'Walkies', he lies down! The only thing he's good at is stuffing himself with biscuits!"

Mum glanced at Whiffer, who had dozed off to sleep. "Well there's seven more weeks, he's bound to improve."

"Seven?" Bertie groaned. Seven more weeks of Miss Bowser shouting and Whiffer coming bottom of the class. He didn't know if he could stand it.

"And you didn't tell me there'd be a test," he grumbled. "Whiffer's got to pass his ODD."

"His what?" asked Mum.

"ODD. Obedient Dog Diploma," said

Bertie. "That's what she gives you."

"Good," said Mum. "With what it's costing me I'll expect him to pass."

Bertie looked doubtful. "Well," he said. "I wouldn't bet on it."

Mum had an idea. "How about this?" she said. "I'll offer you a reward. If Whiffer passes I will double your pocket money."

Bertie looked up. "Really?"

"Really."

Bertie did a quick calculation. Double pocket money that would be … um … double what he usually got, which came to quite a lot. He could buy loads of things with twice the pocket money.

There was just one major problem. There was more chance of Whiffer passing his *driving test* than his Dog Diploma.

CHAPTER 3

Every week for the next six weeks
Bertie dragged Whiffer along to Miss
Bowser's classes. Whiffer showed no
signs of progress. He made friends with
a boxer called Bonzo. He learned to
steal biscuits from Bertie's pocket. But
he didn't learn to obey. Bertie was in
despair. At school he explained the

problem to Donna. Donna had a
hamster and a goldfish so she knew
about pets. She suggested they take
Whiffer to the park for extra lessons.

"It's no use," moaned Bertie, after
Whiffer had gone charging off for the
umpteenth time. "Let's face it, he's never
going to pass."

"Maybe you're just doing it wrong,"
said Donna.

"How can I be? I'm shouting just like
she does."

Whiffer came racing up. He'd
found a mangy old rubber ball
in the grass.

"Try one more time. Tell him
to sit," said Donna.

"SIT!" yelled Bertie.
"WHIFFER, SIT!"

Dirty Bertie

Whiffer dropped the ball at Bertie's feet and barked. Bertie flopped down on the grass. Whiffer sat down too. Donna looked thoughtful.

"Let's try something else. I'll go over there and you come when I call you."

"Me?" said Bertie. "It's not me we're meant to be training!"

Donna looked at him. "Do you want my help or not?"

Bertie sighed. Donna could be very bossy when she wanted to be.

"Ready?" said Donna. "OK. Come!" Bertie walked over to her and Whiffer trotted behind. Donna looked pleased.

"Now roll over," she said.

"Who?"

"You! Go on, do it!"

Feeling pretty stupid, Bertie lay down

and rolled over. Whiffer barked joyfully and rolled over too. This was a great game.

"See! I was right," laughed Donna. "He does whatever you do. All you have to do is get him to copy you!"

"Wow!" said Bertie. "You're a genius!"

"I know," said Donna modestly.

Bertie still looked worried. "But what about the test?" he asked. "It's not just rolling over, there'll be tunnels and fences and stuff."

"Easy!" shrugged Donna. "You just do it with him. Trust me. It'll work."

The following Friday Miss Bowser's class gathered for their final exam. Bertie eyed the other dogs – Bonzo the boxer, Trixie the terrier and Dodie the Dalmatian. They had all been washed and combed for their big day.

Out in the park was a doggy obstacle course. There were tiny hurdles, poles to weave through and a long blue tunnel. Miss Bowser had her clipboard and pencil at the ready to mark each dog's performance. Whiffer tugged at his lead. Over on the other side of the park he'd spotted some boys playing frisbee. Frisbee was his favourite game.

Dodie was first to be tested. She scored top marks, 10 out of 10 with no refusals. Bertie watched Bonzo and Trixie complete the course with flying colours too.

Whiffer didn't seem to be paying attention. He kept staring across the park.

Finally it was Bertie's turn. "OK, Whiffer," he whispered. "Just follow me." He set off at a run and cleared the first hurdle.

Miss Bowser waved her clipboard. "No, no, Bertie! The dog, not you!"

But Donna's plan was working. Whiffer copied Bertie, stepping over the hurdles and clearing the jump like a racehorse. Bertie got down on his hands and knees to crawl through the tunnel.

Dirty Bertie

He danced in and out of the poles as everyone watched in amazement. Almost there! Suddenly a red frisbee whizzed by and hit him on the head.

Whiffer barked excitedly. A frisbee meant a game. *Uh oh*, thought Bertie and grabbed it before Whiffer could pounce. A boy in a football shirt ran up.

"Hey! That's ours!" he said.

Bertie meant to throw it back, but like most frisbees this one had a mind of its own. It took off and curved back over his head. It zoomed over the line of waiting dogs like a low-flying jet. Fifteen pairs of eyes watched it go. Fifteen dogs barked and leaped in the air, straining at their leads. Whiffer saw the frisbee coming back his way. He leaped high, caught it in his mouth and set off like a

Dirty Bertie

greyhound. Before you could shout
"Stay!" the other dogs were after him.

"Yikes!" cried Bertie, dodging out of
the way as the pack thundered past.
Dogs flattened Miss Bowser's hurdles.
Dogs swarmed like rats through the blue
tunnel. Miss Bowser tried to stop them.
She held up her hand like a policeman
stopping the traffic. "SIT!" she yelled.
Bonzo leaped at her and she vanished in
the scrum.

CHAPTER 4

It took some time for all the dogs to be rounded up. The frisbee was returned to its owners slightly chewed at the edges. The blue tunnel had somehow got ripped. But what Bertie didn't understand was why everyone blamed him!

"It wasn't my frisbee!" he pointed out.

"I could've been killed getting bashed on the head like that. Instead of blaming me, you should be asking if I'm all right!"

Miss Bowser did not seem to care if Bertie was all right. She had grass in her hair and muddy paw prints all over her skirt. She said they would get on with the awards so everyone could go home.

Bertie watched gloomily as each dog and his owner went forwards. He doubted if Whiffer would be getting his Diploma, not after all the fuss there'd been.

"And finally…" said Miss Bowser. "Bertie and Whiffer."

Bertie trooped out to the front. Miss Bowser glared at him.

"In twenty years I have never met a dog I couldn't train," she said. "Until now."

She lowered her voice. "However, I

will give you this on one condition. That you promise you will never ever come to one of my classes again."

"Oh, I won't," said Bertie. "Honestly."

"Very well," said Miss Bowser, handing him a piece of paper.

Bertie looked at it.

Obedient Dog Diploma.
Class 1. Awarded to:
Whiffer

"Wow! Thanks!" he said. "Look, Whiffer. You passed!"

Ten minutes later Bertie ran over to the car park where his mum was waiting.

"Look, Mum!" he cried. "We did it! Whiffer passed!"

Mum was delighted. She handed Bertie his pocket money – double his usual amount. "Well done, Bertie. And clever old Whiffer, I told you he could do it!" She glanced behind Bertie. "Where is he, by the way?"

Bertie looked round just in time to catch sight of Whiffer racing across the field. He called out to him.

"Whiffer! Here, boy! Come!"

Whiffer didn't even look back.

Obedient Dog Diploma.
Class 1. Awarded to:
Whiffer

To Joel ~ D R
For my dear Sally x ~ A M

Contents

MONSTER!

CHAPTER 1

Miss Boot glared at her class, waiting for silence.

"The Summer Fair is only a week away, and I need polite, sensible children to help run the stalls," she said. Her eyes fell on Bertie, who was drawing on the back of his hand. She sighed – he was about as sensible as a fruit bat.

Dirty Bertie

Bertie put down his felt-tip pen and sat forwards. There was only one stall he and his friends were interested in running, and he hoped that no one else pinched it.

"I've made a list of all the stalls," said Miss Boot. "Raise your hand if you would like to help with one of them. First, the book stall…"

Bertie waited as Miss Boot worked her way down the list.

"Next, face painting," she said.

Bertie's hand flew into the air. Darren and Eugene leaped out of their seats excitedly.

"Ooh! Ooh, Miss! Can we do it? Can we?" they begged.

"We'd be brilliant at face painting," said Bertie.

Miss Boot sucked in her breath. She imagined entrusting Bertie with a set of face paints. He'd probably give people revolting spots or ugly warts. In no time there'd be a queue of wailing children and angry parents demanding their money back. It was out of the question.

"I don't think that's a good idea," she said. "Donna and Pamela, I'm sure I could rely on you."

"But what about us?" moaned Bertie.

Dirty Bertie

"I have another job for you," said Miss Boot. "The Lucky Dip – you can't do any damage with that."

THE LUCKY DIP? NO! Bertie slumped back in his seat. Why did they always get the most boring stall at the fair? There was nothing to do on the Lucky Dip and the prizes were rubbish. Last year Bertie had won a bar of scented soap – what was "lucky" about that? Besides, he was brilliant at face painting.

When the bell rang for break, Bertie trailed outside with his friends.

"It's not fair," he complained. "We never get chosen for anything!"

"The Lucky Dip… BOR-ING!" groaned Darren.

Dirty Bertie

"Well, there's nothing we can do. Miss Boot won't change her mind," sighed Eugene.

"We're not beaten yet," said Bertie.

He'd set his heart on face painting and he wasn't giving up without a fight. After all, anything could happen on the day. With a bit of luck, Donna and Pamela might be allergic to face paints.

CHAPTER 2

The day of the Summer Fair arrived.
Miss Boot stood at the school gates,
greeting people as they came in. The
sun was shining and the school field was
packed with visitors. Everyone seemed
to be having fun – everyone except
Bertie and his friends at the Lucky Dip.

Bertie sat kicking his feet behind a

large black bin filled with sawdust.

"LUCKY DIP – A PRIZE EVERY TIME!" said the sign. So far they'd only had two customers – one had won a plastic key ring and the other a jar of elastic bands.

"This is rubbish," grumbled Darren.

Bertie gazed longingly at the face-painting stall, where a queue of children waited their turn. Donna was painting someone as a mermaid while Pamela drew a butterfly on a toddler's cheek.

"Look at that," said Bertie in disgust. "They're not even doing it properly!"

"Maybe we could ask them to swap?" suggested Eugene.

Dirty Bertie

"Fat chance!" snorted Darren. "Who wants to run the Lucky Dip? The prizes are all useless!"

Suddenly Bertie had an idea. What if the Lucky Dip prizes weren't so useless? What if it was a gold mine and everyone wanted a go? Then Donna and Pamela might be tempted to swap with them!

"Lend me a pound, Eugene," said Bertie.

"What?"

"Come on," said Bertie. "Do you want to do face painting or not?"

Reluctantly Eugene handed over one of the coins he'd brought for the fair. Bertie wrapped the coin in red tissue paper and hid it near the top of the bin.

A few minutes later Royston Rich stopped at the stall.

Dirty Bertie

"Lucky Dip – a prize every time!"
cried Bertie. "Try your luck, Royston!"

Royston handed over his money and
plunged his hand into the sawdust.

"The best prizes are near the top,"
Bertie whispered.

Dirty Bertie

Royston pulled out a ball of red tissue paper. He unwrapped it to reveal Eugene's shiny pound coin.

"WOW! I won a pound!" he cried.

"That's nothing," said Bertie. "Don't tell anyone, but there's a fortune in here — maybe a hundred pounds!"

"Never!" gasped Royston.

"Don't say I told you," whispered Bertie.

Royston quickly paid for another go. This time he won a pencil sharpener, but it didn't put him off. He rushed off to tell his friends.

"ONE HUNDRED POUNDS?" cried Darren. "You made that up!"

"Of course I did, but Royston doesn't know that," said Bertie. "You wait, soon everyone will want a go. Then we'll see if Donna and Pamela want to swap."

Bertie was right. Once word got around that the Lucky Dip was a treasure trove, it began to draw a crowd. Children queued in the hope of finding a five or ten pound note. Eventually Donna and Pamela came over to see what the fuss was about.

Dirty Bertie

"What's going on?" asked Pamela.

"Royston won a pound," Bertie explained. "It turns out the Lucky Dip's full of money."

"Really?" said Donna.

"Yes, we've won quite a bit ourselves," said Bertie. "Haven't we, Eugene?"

Dirty Bertie

"Oh … er, yes, we have," said Eugene.

"Millions!" said Darren.

"Wow!" said Pamela. "I wish Miss Boot had given us the Lucky Dip!"

Bertie pretended to consider. "Well, I suppose we could swap stalls for a bit," he offered generously.

Pamela and Donna looked at each other.

"Could we?" asked Donna. "But what about Miss Boot?"

"She won't care!" said Bertie. "She's too busy to notice."

"Okay, you're on," said Pamela.

Bertie smiled to himself. *At last!* he thought. Now was his chance to show what could really be done with a set of face paints!

CHAPTER 3

"This is wicked," said Darren. "I just turned Royston Rich into a rat!"

"And I gave Angela Nicely measles," said Eugene. "She loved it!"

Bertie and his friends had been busy. So far they hadn't painted any mermaids, fairies or butterflies – instead they had done two pirates, a werewolf and a ghost.

Bertie nudged Darren. "Look, there's Know-All Nick," he said. "Let's paint him."

"Yes," grinned Darren. "We could make him really UGLY."

"He's ugly already," said Eugene.

Know-All Nick caught sight of the stall and stopped.

"Face painting?" he smirked. "I thought Miss Boot put you on the Lucky Dip."

"She did, but we swapped," said Bertie. "Why don't we paint you, Nick?"

"No thanks," replied Nick. "My mum says I've got sensitive skin."

"It's okay, these are extra-sensitive face paints," said Bertie.

"I bet you'd look great with your face painted," said Darren.

"You think so?" said Nick.

Dirty Bertie

"Oh yes, with a face like yours you could be anything," said Eugene. "A superhero, for instance."

Nick's eyes lit up. Secretly he'd always believed he'd make a fantastic superhero. He could be TIDYMAN – saving the world from smelly socks and pants.

He narrowed his eyes. "But how do I know you won't play a trick on me?" he asked.

"US?" said Bertie. "As if we'd do that!"

"So what's it to be?" asked Darren. "A wizard or a superhero?"

Nick shook his head. "Make me a lion," he said. "A big scary lion."

Bertie raised his eyebrows. He couldn't think of anyone *less* like a lion than Nick – he was more of a slug or a worm. In any case, a lion wasn't much of a challenge. Nick deserved something better, something special. Wait, he had it – the perfect idea. People would certainly get a fright when they saw Nick's face. Bertie whispered to his friends, who grinned and nodded.

"What are you saying?" whined Nick.

"Nothing!" said Bertie. "We'll make you a lion. Close your eyes so you don't get paint in them."

Nick sat down and did as he was told.

"Right, let's get started," said Bertie. He reached for the green and daubed it all over Nick's face.

"What are you doing?" demanded Nick.

"Just putting on the base colour," replied Bertie. "Golden for a lion."

"Don't forget the whiskers," said Nick.

"Don't worry," said Bertie. "I won't."

He reached for another face paint and gave Nick thick black eyebrows. Next he added ugly scars running across his forehead.

"Do I look like a lion?" asked Nick.

"Definitely," grinned Eugene. "A *monster* lion."

Finally Bertie wet Nick's hair and
shaped it into jagged peaks.

"This is your lion's mane," he said.
"There we are – finished!"

He stood back to admire his work.

"Oh, yes!" said Eugene. "The Lion King!"

"Dead scary!" said Darren.

Nick stood up. Bertie had thought
Nick was ugly before, but now he made

Dracula seem handsome.

"Where's the mirror? I want to see myself!" cried Nick.

"Oh, um, sorry, Darren broke the mirror," said Bertie, hiding it behind his back.

"But we promise you won't be disappointed," said Darren.

Nick showed his claws. "Am I really scary?" he asked.

"Very scary," said Bertie. "Why don't you creep up on someone and give them a fright?"

"I'm going to!" said Nick. "You watch, I'm going to creep up and roar. GRRRR!"

"Oh, help, help! It's a lion!" whimpered Bertie. "That'll be fifty pence, please."

Nick paid and went off looking pleased with his new look.

Eugene laughed. "He's not going to be too happy when he sees himself."

"No, not when he finds out he looks like Frankenstein's monster," said Darren.

"Well, if you ask me, I think it's a big improvement," said Bertie.

CHAPTER 4

Nick made his way through the crowds.
People turned to stare as he went past.
A toddler saw him and burst into tears.

*Anyone would think they'd never seen
a lion before!* thought Nick. He practised
his roar under his breath. "ROOARR!"

Who should he sneak up on first?
Trevor or maybe Royston Rich? No,

they'd both pretend they weren't scared.
What he wanted was someone who'd
really scream with fright. Come to think
of it, his mum could scream quite loudly.
He spotted her at the refreshment stall,
chatting with Miss Boot over a cup of tea.

Perfect, thought Nick. *Wait till a lion
creeps up and pounces on them.*

Back at their stall, Bertie and his friends
watched as Nick slunk over to the
refreshment stall and dropped down on
all fours.

"What's he doing now?" asked Eugene.

"Pretending to be a lion," said Darren.

"Maybe he's creeping up on someone,"
said Bertie. "Wait, isn't that Miss Boot?"

"Yes," said Eugene. "And she's talking

Dirty Bertie

to Nick's mum."

Surely Nick wasn't planning to scare his mum and Miss Boot?

"Come on!" said Bertie, hurrying over. "I wouldn't miss this for anything."

As they reached the refreshment stall, they were just in time to see Nick crawl under his mum's table.

"I'm so glad Nicholas is doing well," Nick's mum was saying. "He's such a kind and sensible boy…"

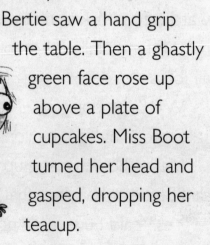 Bertie saw a hand grip the table. Then a ghastly green face rose up above a plate of cupcakes. Miss Boot turned her head and gasped, dropping her teacup.

Dirty Bertie

"GRAAAARR!" roared Nick.

"EEEK!" screamed his mum, falling backwards off her chair.

Know-All Nick jumped out, growling and showing his teeth.

"GRRRR! GRAAAARR!"

Miss Boot stared at the monster. She knew that face.

"NICHOLAS!" she thundered. "IS THIS YOUR IDEA OF A JOKE?"

"Did I scare you?" cried Know-All Nick.

"Good heavens, Nicholas! What have you done to your face?" gasped his mum.

"It's face paint," said Nick. "I'm a lion! GRRRR!"

"A lion indeed!" snorted Miss Boot. "I've never heard such nonsense. Take a look at yourself!"

She grabbed her handbag and brought out a pocket mirror. Nick stared at his reflection in horror.

"But … I look like FRANKENSTEIN'S MONSTER!" he wailed.

"Yes," said Miss Boot. "I'm surprised at you, Nicholas. And Donna and Pamela should be ashamed."

"But it wasn't Donna and Pamela," moaned Nick. "It was Bertie! He tricked me! He said I was a big scary lion."

"BERTIE?" barked Miss Boot. "I warned

him to keep away from the face paints!
Where is that wretched boy?"

She looked around. But there was no
sign of Bertie or his friends – not at the
face-painting stall or anywhere else.

Bertie had heard Miss Boot bawl his
name and had legged it back to the
Lucky Dip to hide. He peeped out of
the bin. All in all, the Summer Fair hadn't
turned out so badly. He was looking
forward to seeing Know-All Nick on
Monday. Perhaps from now on they
should just call him Nickenstein…

LUCKY DIP
A PRIZE
EVERY
50P TIME

BUSKERS!

CHAPTER 1

It was Saturday morning and Bertie was out shopping with Mum and Suzy. He couldn't see the point of shopping, unless it involved sweets or toys. Today, however, Suzy needed new school shoes. He trailed behind them along the high street. *Is anything more boring than shoe shopping?* he thought.

Dirty Bertie

The sound
of music drifted
down the street.
Outside a shop,
a man was
tootling away
on some sort
of instrument.
Bertie stopped
in his tracks.
"It's just
a busker," said
Mum. "Come
on, Bertie, we
don't have
time."

Bertie didn't hear – he had already wandered over to take a closer look.

BOOM, CHIKKA, BOOM!

The busker had a drum machine tapping out a tinny rhythm.

But something else had caught Bertie's eye. Lying on the pavement was a hat – a hat full of money! As Bertie stared, someone dropped fifty pence into the hat as they went by. Bertie could hardly believe it. He'd seen people throw coins in a fountain, but never a hat before! Perhaps it was a lucky hat? He stooped down to pick it up.

"Look at this!" he called to Suzy.

The music came to a sudden halt.

"Hey, you! Get your thieving hands off!" cried the busker.

Mum came running over.

"What are you doing?" she hissed,
snatching the hat from Bertie.

"I'm so sorry," she said, handing it back
to the busker. "I'm sure he wasn't going
to keep it."

"Why not?" asked Bertie. "It was just
lying there!"

Mum grabbed Bertie by the arm and
marched him off.

"What?" said Bertie. "I was only looking at it!"

Suzy rolled her eyes. "You are *so* embarrassing," she groaned.

At the shoe shop, Bertie fidgeted while Suzy tried on endless pairs of shoes.

"How was I to know the hat was his?" he grumbled.

"Why do you think he left it there?" asked Mum.

"Don't ask me," said Bertie. "It's a stupid place to leave a hat!"

"It's there to collect the money!" explained Mum. "Buskers play on the street. If you like the music then you drop money in their hat."

"What? Just for blowing a trumpet?"

said Bertie.

"It was a saxophone," sighed Suzy. "And actually he was pretty good."

Bertie stared. Wait a minute… So you could play music on the street and people would actually pay you? Why hadn't someone told him this before?

"Can anyone do busking?" he asked.

"No, you have to be able to play an instrument," said Suzy.

"I can play," said Bertie. "I used to play the recorder."

"Yes, until you broke it," said Mum.

"Well, I bet I could play the saxophone," said Bertie. "Our music teacher says I must be good at something."

"Whatever she says, you're not going busking," said Mum firmly.

Dirty Bertie

"Why not?" asked Bertie.

"Because you're way too young!" said Mum.

Bertie sighed. He didn't see what his age had got to do with it. He bet Darren and Eugene wouldn't think he was too young. Come to think of it, why didn't they all go busking together? With three of them they could make an almighty racket! They were bound to earn a fortune!

CHAPTER 2

The shopping trip was a failure. Suzy couldn't find any school shoes she liked and by eleven o'clock they were back home. Bertie rang Darren and Eugene and invited them round, eager to tell them his latest idea.

"BUSKING?" said Darren. "You must be joking!"

"Why not?" said Bertie. "All you do is put down a hat and people give you money. It's easy!"

"Yes, if you're a busker," said Eugene.

"We don't even play instruments," Darren pointed out.

"We do," argued Bertie. "Eugene plays the violin."

"I'm *learning* the violin," Eugene corrected him. "I've only had a few lessons."

"And who's going to pay to listen to us?" asked Darren.

"Loads of people," said Bertie. "You could play the drums and I can sing and play my kazoo."

Bertie had got a plastic kazoo in his Christmas stocking. It was easy to play – you just had to blow and hum at the

same time. For a few weeks he'd driven
his family up the wall.

"Anyway, we don't know
any songs," said Eugene.

"That's why we're going to
practise," said Bertie. "You
fetch your violin and I'll find a
drum for Darren."

A little later a deafening noise came
from Bertie's room. Eugene screeched on
his violin while Darren bashed a biscuit tin
with two wooden spoons. Bertie yelled
out the words, sometimes breaking off to
play a solo on his kazoo.

"*Jingle bells, jingle bells…*
Doo doo doo doo-doo
Oh what fun it is to…"

The door flew open. Bertie's dad stood
there glaring.

"What's all the noise?" he demanded.

"We're practising," said Bertie. "Did you like it?"

"Like it? It sounds like someone's being murdered!" said Dad. "You've even driven Whiffer out of the house."

Bertie waved his kazoo. "We've got to practise," he said.

"What for?" asked Dad.

"So we can go busking," Bertie replied.

"You need a licence to go busking," said Dad. "Now please, pack it in. I'm trying to work."

He slammed the door.

Bertie's kazoo dribbled spit down his jumper. *Typical*, he thought. His parents went on and on at him to learn an instrument and when he did, they just complained!

CHAPTER 3

Darren and Eugene stayed for lunch.

"Mum, can we go busking this afternoon?" Bertie asked, sitting down at the table.

"Certainly not," said Mum. "We've been over this already."

"Pleeeease!" begged Bertie. "Not in town, just at the shops down the road."

"No, you're too young!" said Mum.

Darren reached for some crisps.
"Bertie reckons we could make a
fortune," he said.

"Does he now?" said Mum. "Well, he
can dream on because you're not going."

Bertie threw back his head in despair.
It was so unfair! All that practising for
nothing! If they couldn't go busking, they
might as well give up and go to the park.
Wait a minute, thought Bertie. The park
was on the way to the shops – and if
they happened to take their instruments,
who was going to know?

After lunch, they crept downstairs and
tiptoed to the door.

"BERTIE!" called Mum. "Where do
you think you're going?"

Uh-oh.

Dirty Bertie

"Just to the park!" Bertie shouted.

Mum came into the hall.

"Why are you all wearing your coats?" she asked.

"It's cold!" said Bertie.

"It's the middle of June!" said Mum.

"Yes, but we need them for goalposts," said Darren, thinking quickly.

The others nodded in agreement.

Mum narrowed her eyes.

Dirty Bertie

"Okay," she said. "But make sure you're back by four."

The three of them hurried out of the front door. Once they were down the road, they unzipped their coats. Eugene brought out his violin, and a biscuit tin and some spoons fell out of Darren's jacket. Bertie took his kazoo from his pocket.

"We made it," he said. "Let's get down the shops before anyone sees us."

Dirty Bertie

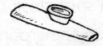

It was a bright summer's day and the local high street was busy. At the coffee shop customers sat outside, enjoying the sunshine. All was calm and peaceful.

Eugene fiddled nervously with his violin bow. He'd never played in public before.

"Can't we go somewhere a bit less busy?" he asked.

"No, this is perfect," said Bertie.

"If we see anyone we know, I'm not doing it," warned Darren.

"Stop worrying, it'll be fine!" said Bertie. "Who's got the hat?"

Eugene pulled a woolly hat from his pocket.

"We'll start over there," said Bertie, pointing to the café.

They chose a spot close by and placed the hat on the ground. The buskers could only play three songs and Bertie didn't know all the words, but he doubted that anyone would notice.

"Ready?" he said. "One, two, three..."

"Twinkle twinkle, little star,
How I ... doo-doo doo-doo dooo!"

Outside the café people looked up, startled. One minute they were enjoying the peace and quiet, the next it was shattered by three scruffy children making a terrible din. Some of the customers covered their ears. A baby in a buggy started to howl.

"What a row!" moaned the mother, rocking the buggy back and forth. "Please, somebody make them stop!"

A door banged
open and the
café manager
stormed out.
"What
do you think
you're doing?" he
demanded.

"Busking," said
Bertie. "It's like music on the street."

"I know what it is, but you can't do it
here," snapped the manager. "Clear off!"

He waved an arm at them and went
back inside.

Bertie frowned. He had expected a bit
more enthusiasm.

"Come on, let's go to the park,"
suggested Eugene, relieved.

"At least we gave it a try," said Darren.

"But we haven't earned any money yet!" protested Bertie.

"You heard him. The manager told us to clear off!" said Darren.

Bertie looked at their audience. Maybe they'd started with the wrong song?

"Let's play 'Jingle Bells'," he suggested. "Everyone likes that. It makes you think of Christmas."

"But it's summer," said Eugene. The trouble with Bertie was he never knew when to give up.

"*Jingle bells, jingle bells!*
Doo doo, doo doo-doo!"

People at the café finished their drinks and left in a hurry.

"*Oh what fun it is to ride…*"

"STOP!" yelled the manager.

The music stumbled to a halt.

Dirty Bertie

"What did I tell you?" cried the manager. "You're driving all my customers away!"

Bertie looked around. The café did seem a little emptier than when they'd first arrived.

"Shall we play something else?" he asked.

"NO!" said the manager. "Just go! Find someone else to annoy!"

Bertie sighed and picked up the woolly hat. He held it out.

"I don't suppose you've got any spare change?"

CHAPTER 4

Further down the street, the three of them sat down on a bench.

"It's not fair!" grumbled Bertie. "We haven't earned a single penny."

"I told you we were wasting our time," said Eugene. "We might as well give up and go to the park."

But Bertie didn't admit defeat so easily.

Dirty Bertie

They were just starting to get the hang of busking.

On the square in front of them, children were running around while people sat on benches in the sun. It looked like an ideal spot for busking.

"Let's set up here," said Bertie.

The other two groaned.

"Face it, Bertie, this is never going to work!" said Darren.

"Just one last try, then we'll call it a day," promised Bertie.

They picked up their instruments again.

Bertie wiped the dribble off his kazoo and counted them in.

"One, two, three…"

BOOM, CHIKKA, BOOM!

Bertie looked up. Across the square was the busker he'd seen in town earlier. His drum machine blared out as he began playing the saxophone.

"He can't do that!" complained Bertie. "This is our spot."

"But he can actually play," said Eugene.

"Maybe," said Bertie. "But there's three of us. I bet we can play louder!"

They launched into the last song on their playlist:

"The wheels on the bus go…"

BASH, BASH, BASH!

Darren thumped his drum.

"HEY!"

The busker had turned off his drum machine. He marched across the square towards them.

Dirty Bertie

"You again!" he said to Bertie. "What do you think you're playing at?"

"'The Wheels on the Bus'," replied Bertie.

"Well, cut it out! This is my pitch, find your own," snapped the busker.

He stomped back to his place, switched on the drum machine and began again.

Bertie stared. "What a cheek! We were here first!" he grumbled.

"We can't compete with that," said Darren. "It's proper music!"

"*Please*, let's just go to the park!" begged Eugene.

But Bertie certainly wasn't giving up without a fight. Why should *they* be the ones to leave? If anyone should go, it was the busker – he was trying to pinch their audience!

"Start again and play louder," said Bertie.

They began playing. The busker glared and turned up his drum machine to full volume. Bertie yelled even louder to try and drown him out.

"THE HORN ON THE BUS GOES BEEP BEEP BEEP!"

Eugene's violin screeched. Darren bashed the biscuit tin so hard he put a dent in it. People around the square grabbed their children and fled to get away from the noise.

"OKAY, STOP! STOP!"

Dirty Bertie

The busker was back, waving his arms in front of them.

"I thought I told you to beat it!" he said.

"We were here first," replied Bertie.

"You were not!"

"We were so!"

"Look, you're just kids," said the busker. "I do this for a living. Why don't you just run along home, eh?"

Bertie folded his arms stubbornly.

The busker looked around. He was losing his audience fast.

"I'll give you a pound," he said, in desperation.

Bertie raised his eyebrows. "You mean a pound each?" he asked.

"No! Oh, all right, if you promise to clear off and never come back," said the busker.

Three pounds! It wasn't a fortune but it was better than nothing.

"Come on, let's go to the sweet shop," said Darren.

They set off back along the street, but just as they reached the sweet shop,

Dirty Bertie

Bertie heard a voice he knew.

"BERTIE!"

Oh no – his mum and Suzy! Hadn't they done enough shopping for one day?

Mum spotted their instruments before they could hide them. She glared. "I thought you were going to the park?"

"We were…" said Bertie weakly.

"And what have you got there?" demanded Mum.

Bertie opened his hand to reveal the three pound coins.

"So despite everything I said, you went busking," said Mum. "I'll take the money, thank you. We'll give it to someone who deserves it."

They watched as she marched off down the street and stopped at the busker playing the saxophone. She

Dirty Bertie

dropped the coins into his hat.

Bertie put his head in his hands.

"*Now* can we go to the park?" groaned
Eugene.

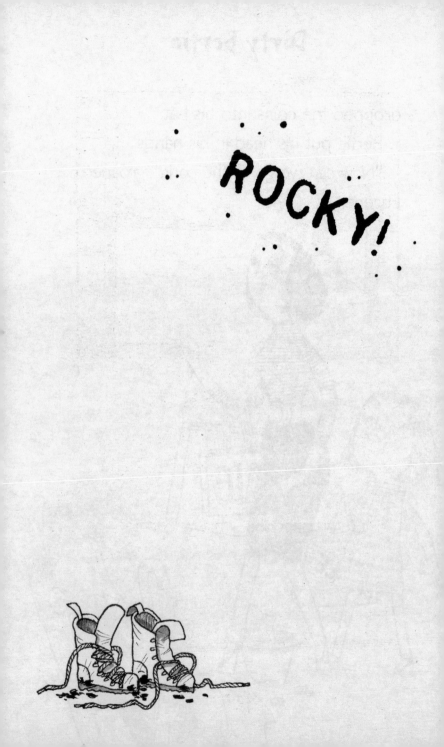

CHAPTER 1

"Come on, everybody up! The sun's shining!" cried Dad, throwing open the curtains.

Mum groaned. Suzy hid under her duvet. Bertie sat up and blinked. *Where am I?* he thought. *This isn't my bedroom!* Then he remembered – they were staying in a youth hostel. Dad had dragged them away for a weekend in the middle of nowhere.

"It's a beautiful day and we're surrounded by nature," said Dad. "Look out there – hills, trees, sheep!"

Bertie yawned. He'd seen sheep before and they had trees in the local park.

"We're not going on a *walk*, are we?" groaned Suzy.

"Better than that," said Dad. "We're going on an adventure!"

Bertie's eyes lit up. "You mean you're taking us to GO WILD!" he said.

He'd seen a poster for Go Wild! in the entrance hall. They had walkways and rope bridges, and you could swoop through the treetops on a zip wire like Tarzan. It looked amazing!

"Who needs theme parks?" said Dad.
"We've got all the thrills we need right
here. We're going to climb Craggy Peak!"

"Craggy what?" asked Suzy.

"Craggy Peak – it's a mountain," Dad
explained.

"You're not serious!" said Mum. "Surely
we should stick to climbing hills?"

"Bertie can't even climb a tree!"
hooted Suzy.

"I can!" cried Bertie. He was brilliant at climbing trees, although getting down again was another matter.

"Don't worry," said Dad. "Anyone can climb Craggy Peak. There's an easy path that takes you right to the top."

"It's still a mountain," argued Mum. "What about the children?"

"It'll be good for them," said Dad.

"But we don't have the right gear," grumbled Suzy.

"Ah, that's where you're wrong," said Dad. He pulled out a large orange rucksack from under the bed. "I've brought everything we need. I've been planning this as a surprise!"

Bertie rolled his eyes. If his dad really wanted to surprise them, why didn't he take them to Disneyland?

"What's the point of climbing a mountain?" he moaned.

"To get to the top, of course!" replied Dad. "Think of it as an adventure. We'll be like Scott of the Antarctic!"

"Isn't he the one that never came back?" said Mum grimly.

CHAPTER 2

Dad pulled into the car park and everyone climbed out.

"There it is!" cried Dad. "Craggy Peak!"

Bertie stared. Beyond the fields was a huge grey mountain. It was so high the peak was hidden in mist.

"We're not climbing that!" he groaned.

Dirty Bertie

"It'll be fun," said Dad. "Just think, you'll be able to tell your friends that you've actually climbed a mountain!"

Bertie thought he'd rather tell his friends that he'd actually been to Go Wild!

Dad opened the boot and hauled out the rucksack, staggering under its weight.

"What have you *got* in there?" asked Mum.

"Like I said, everything we need," replied Dad. "Maps, compass, hats, gloves, waterproofs, first-aid kit and plenty of water."

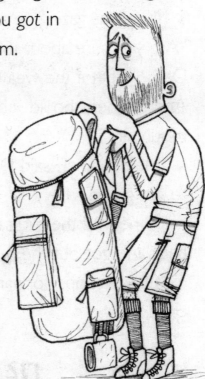

"No biscuits?" asked Bertie.

Dad shook his head. "We've got a packed lunch from the youth hostel. Sandwiches, apples and energy bars."

Bertie plunged his hands in his pockets. They'd probably starve to death! Who in their right mind climbed a mountain without a packet of biscuits?

Mum was gazing up at Craggy Peak. "Are you sure about this?" she asked Dad. "What if the weather changes? And besides, should *you* be going up a mountain?"

"Me? I'm fine!" said Dad. "I can't wait to get going!"

He heaved the rucksack on to his back and got out the map.

"Okay, troops, forward march!" he cried.

They climbed over a stile to reach a
muddy track winding uphill.

"Race you to the top!" cried Suzy.

"Last one's a smelly slug," said Bertie.

"DON'T RUN! Save your energy!"
warned Dad. But Bertie and Suzy were
already racing on ahead.

Dirty Bertie

An hour later they stopped by a stone wall. Dad took off the rucksack and dumped it on the ground.

"I need a rest!" he groaned, sitting on a tree stump.

"Already?" said Bertie. "I'm not even tired!"

Mountain climbing was turning out to be more fun than he'd expected. He'd already jumped in some sheep poo and sunk up to his ankles in a muddy bog.

He'd even found a good poking stick that was great for annoying Suzy. All in all, things were looking up!

Mum and Dad, on the other hand, looked worn out. They were both sweating and red in the face. Dad kept grumbling that his new boots hurt and the rucksack weighed a ton.

"Are we nearly there?" asked Bertie. He'd lost sight of the mountain top.

"Not yet," said Dad.

He studied the map for a moment, frowning. He tried turning it the other way up.

"Hmm. Uh-huh. Mmm," he mumbled.

"We're not lost, are we?" asked Mum anxiously.

"Lost? Of course not!" snorted Dad. "It's just a case of finding the right path."

"Where *is* the right path?" asked Suzy.

They had been following a path, but a while back it had divided into two. Dad had decided the left path was right (which sounded wrong). Now there was no sign of any path at all.

"It must be straight on," Dad said, folding the map.

Dirty Bertie

"*Up there?*" asked Mum. The rocks and boulders above looked gigantic.

"The path must be overgrown. I'm sure we'll find it," said Dad.

Mum glanced at the sky. "It looks like rain," she muttered. "That's all we need."

"Can I run on ahead and climb the rocks?" pleaded Bertie.

"No, stay with us," said Dad. "I don't want you getting into trouble."

Bertie sighed. He didn't see how he could get into any trouble. They were on a mountain in the middle of nowhere – what could possibly happen?

CHAPTER 3

The sky had grown darker. The wind beat against them as they clambered over the rocks. Bertie was out in front and hauled himself up. If this was the path, it was obviously made for mountain goats! Not that he minded. Climbing Craggy Peak was more exciting than he'd expected. Bertie imagined he

Dirty Bertie

was a famous explorer trekking through
snow and watching out for polar bears.
He stopped to wait for the others. After
a few minutes, Suzy and Mum appeared.

"This is fun!" said Bertie.

"You think so?" panted Mum.

"It's an adventure!" said
Bertie. "Are we climbing those
massive rocks up there?"

Mum squinted at
them and frowned.

"This can't be
right," she said.
"And where's your
dad got to?"

"I thought he was with you," said Bertie.

They all looked round. A moment later a voice reached them, echoing from below.

"HEEEEEEEELP!"

Mum groaned. "I knew this would happen!" she said.

"What? He hasn't lost the sandwiches, has he?" asked Bertie.

"No," said Mum. "We'd better go back and help."

They found Dad further down on the rocks. He was standing on a narrow ledge, gripping the rock he was facing. He seemed to be hanging on for dear life, even though the drop below was only a couple of metres.

"You all right, Dad?" asked Bertie,

Dirty Bertie

looking down on him.

"Do I look all right? I CAN'T MOVE!" moaned Dad.

"Yes, you can," said Bertie. "You just have to let go of the rock."

"I CAN'T!" wailed Dad. "I'll fall!"

Bertie and Suzy looked puzzled.

"He's got vertigo," explained Mum. "He's scared of heights. Don't you remember the time he went on the big wheel at the funfair?"

Bertie had forgotten. Dad had kept his eyes shut the whole time.

"I warned you," said Mum. "I said this was a bad idea."

Dirty Bertie

"Never mind that, just get me down!" cried Dad.

Bertie couldn't see what Dad was making such a fuss about. He climbed down to the ledge, treading on his hand.

"OWW!" howled Dad.

"Give me your hand, I can pull you up," said Bertie.

Dad shook his head. There was no way he was letting go of the rock. He needed both hands to hang on.

"I know, what if Mum gives you a piggyback?" suggested Bertie.

Suzy gave him a withering look. "Can't we just go back down?" she asked.

"NO! That's even worse!" said Dad.

"Well, what do you want us to do?" asked Mum. "We can't stay here forever!"

Dad shook his head helplessly.

"If we're stopping, can we have our sandwiches?" asked Bertie.

"NO!" shouted everyone at once.

Bertie shrugged. He was only asking. There was no point in going hungry.

Mum tried to ring the youth hostel on her mobile, but there was no signal. Someone would have to go and get help.

"Suzy, you and Bertie go back down while I stay here with Dad," she said.

"I don't mind staying!" offered Bertie. After all, the food was in Dad's rucksack.

"No, you go with Suzy," ordered

Mum. "As soon as you find someone, explain to them what's happened. And be careful!"

"Okay!" sighed Bertie. "*Then* can we have lunch?"

No one answered. Everyone seemed to be in a bad mood. He sighed. This never would have happened if they'd gone to Go Wild! It was difficult to get stuck if you were whizzing down a zip wire.

CHAPTER 4

Bertie followed Suzy as they made their way back down the mountain. Before long they reached the stone wall where they had rested coming up. Further on, they came to the spot where the paths divided. Bertie spotted a group of ramblers coming up the slope.

"Leave the talking to me," said Suzy as

they went to meet them.

"Excuse me!" she said. "Our dad's back there and he's got sort of stuck."

"Oh dear!" said one of the women. "Where is he?"

"On the rocks! He's hanging on by his fingernails!" said Bertie dramatically.

Suzy glared at him to shut up. "He's stuck on a sort of ledge," she said. "But we can't get him to move."

"Mum says he's got lurgy toes!" added Bertie.

"Good heavens!" gasped the woman.

Suzy sighed. "He means vertigo. But we're not sure what to do – Mum sent us to get help."

"Is he in any danger?" asked one of the men.

"Well, not really," said Suzy.

"He could be," said Bertie. "His legs have gone wobbly so he could fall."

The ramblers looked alarmed. The woman took out her phone.

"I think we'd better call Mountain Rescue," she said. "They'll know what to do. Let's see if I can get a signal."

Mountain Rescue? Bertie thought that sounded fantastic. He didn't even know there *was* a Mountain Rescue!

Bertie and Suzy climbed back up the mountain to their parents.

"Help's on the way," said Suzy.

Half an hour later they heard a loud whirring noise overhead. A blast of wind kicked up the dust. Dad looked up in surprise.

"Oh, you're kidding!" he groaned.

"Why have they sent a helicopter?" cried Mum.

"You told us to get help!" said Bertie.

"Yes, but I didn't mean Mountain Rescue!" said Mum. "Your dad's just scared of heights."

"It's not my fault," said Suzy. "It was

Bertie. He made it sound as if Dad was hanging off a cliff!"

Bertie couldn't see why they were complaining. They'd asked for help and what could be better than Mountain Rescue? Besides, he'd always wanted to go in a helicopter!

The rescue team jumped out. They climbed down to the ledge, bringing ropes, a stretcher and a first-aid kit.

"Are you hurt?" asked the team leader. "Did you fall?"

Dad shook his head.

"Any broken bones?"

"I don't think so," muttered Dad.

"So what's the problem?" asked the woman.

Dad had gone bright pink. He mumbled something about getting stuck.

Dirty Bertie

Dirty Bertie

"He's scared of heights," Mum explained. "He gets vertigo."

"I see," said the team leader. "Maybe you should have thought of that before you climbed a mountain."

They strapped Dad on to the stretcher since he was too shaky to walk. Then the rescue team hauled him up off the ledge and carried him to the helicopter. Mum, Suzy and Bertie followed behind.

"Well, are you coming with us?" asked the rescue team leader.

"Wicked!" said Bertie, peering inside. "Can I sit at the front?"

With a whirr of blades the helicopter lifted into the sky. Bertie was given some sweet tea and a biscuit. He gazed down as they pulled away from the mountain. Wait till he told Darren and Eugene about this!

Minutes later he could see rows of tiny cars in the car park. Further on he spotted a wood with rope bridges, walkways and zip wires. Bertie pointed excitedly.

"Look, there's Go Wild! Can we go tomorrow?" he begged. "Can we, pleeeease?"

Mum groaned. "ANYTHING!" she said. "Just as long as it doesn't involve mountains."

For Nathaniel ~ D R

For Reece Coggan and Tyra Barnes –
thanks for the great story ideas! ~ A M

Contents

CHAPTER 1

Bertie's head flopped forwards. It was Monday assembly and as usual Miss Skinner had been droning on for hours.

"Now," she said. "Listen carefully because Miss Darling has some exciting news."

Miss Darling stood up. "As you know we're nearing the end of term," she said.

Dirty Bertie

"And this year we are holding our very first Pudsley Prom Party!"

Bertie looked up. *What?* A Prom Party? But they always watched a film at the end of the summer term. It was the one thing he looked forward to every year!

"It's going to be heaps of fun," said Miss Darling. "There will be party food and games and prizes. And of course, you can't have a prom without dancing."

Bertie groaned. *Dancing?* YUCK! It sounded like torture! Why couldn't they watch *The Blob from Planet Zog* like last year?

After assembly he trailed back to class with his friends.

Dirty Bertie

"A Prom Party?" he grumbled. "Who wants to go to a stupid prom?"

"Lots of schools have them," said Eugene.

"My cousin arrived at his prom in a massive stretch limo," said Darren.

"Really?" said Bertie.

He wouldn't mind arriving in a limo, as long as he could choose who came in it. Obviously Know-All Nick could walk. But even so, it wouldn't make the prom any more bearable.

Dirty Bertie

"Why's there got to be dancing?" he complained.

Bertie hated dancing. He always trod on people's feet. His mum had once dragged him along to his sister's dance class. Miss Foxtrot had made him wear ballet shoes and prance up and down on tippy toes. He wouldn't be doing that again in a hurry.

"It'll be just like a school disco," said Eugene. "I like dancing."

"Well, I don't," said Bertie. "And I'm not dancing with any girls! No way!"

Darren smiled and glanced at Eugene. "It's a prom, Bertie," he said. "Surely you know about proms?"

Bertie frowned. "Know what?"

"That you *have* to take a girl," said Darren. "Isn't that right, Eugene?"

"Do you?" Eugene gulped. It was news to him.

Darren winked. "Course you do!" he said. "That's the whole point."

Bertie had turned deathly white. Surely they couldn't be serious?

"TAKE A GIRL?" he said, almost choking. "You mean like – you go *together*?"

"Yes," said Darren. "But obviously you have to ask them first."

"ASK THEM?" said Bertie.

"Of course," said Darren. "You'll need a partner or you won't have anyone to dance with! So who are you going to ask?"

Dirty Bertie

Bertie looked as if he might pass out. How could Miss Darling do this to him? She actually expected him to ask a girl to the prom and then dance with her? It was too horrible for words! He felt sick just thinking about it.

"No, no, I can't," he muttered, shaking his head. "I'm not doing it!"

Darren shrugged. "Please yourself, but you'll miss all the games and prizes – and the party food. And you know what they'll make you do if you don't go to the prom?"

"What?" asked Bertie.

"Extra maths with Miss Boot," said Darren.

Bertie stared in disbelief. "Wait a minute," he said. "If we've ALL got to ask a girl, then you'll have to do it too."

Dirty Bertie

"Of course!" said Darren. "We don't mind, do we, Eugene?"

"Erm … no, no problem," said Eugene doubtfully.

Bertie's shoulders drooped. He ducked into the toilets saying he didn't feel well.

Eugene turned to Darren. "Are you serious?" he moaned. "We *really* have to take a *girl*?"

Darren laughed. "Course we don't!" he said. "I only made it up because I knew Bertie would be terrified! I can't believe he actually fell for it."

"You had me worried for a minute there," said Eugene. "But shouldn't we tell him the truth?"

"Are you kidding?" said Darren. "This could be the best joke ever. Imagine Bertie turning up to the prom with a girl. It'll be hilarious!"

CHAPTER 2

For the rest of the day Bertie went around under a dark cloud. How could his classmates carry on as if everything was normal? He needed advice but who could he ask? His friends weren't worried about the prom and his parents would say he was making a fuss about nothing. What about his sister, Suzy?

Dirty Bertie

As soon as he got home, he raced upstairs to her room.

"What do you want?" groaned Suzy.

"I suppose you've heard about this Prom Party?" Bertie said.

"Oh yes, for you younger kids," said Suzy. "Sounds fun."

"Fun!" cried Bertie. "I've just found out we have to bring someone."

Suzy looked puzzled. "Who?"

"A girl!" said Bertie. "You've got to bring a girl or you can't go!"

Suzy raised her eyebrows. "And who told you that?" she asked.

"Darren," said Bertie. "Why? Isn't it true?"

Suzy smiled. It was obvious Bertie's friends were playing a joke on him. Of course she could easily put him out of his misery… On the other hand, this was her bogey-nosed, annoying little brother. It was much funnier to play along.

"Of course it's true," she said. "Everyone takes a partner to a prom."

Bertie sank down on the bed in despair. So Darren was right!

"But I CAN'T! Who can I ask?" he moaned.

Dirty Bertie

"What about the girls in your class?" asked Suzy.

"But they're all … GIRLS!" said Bertie. "I can't ask them!"

Suzy smiled. "Come on, there must be one you like," she teased.

"SHUT UP! THERE ISN'T!" wailed Bertie.

"It's only a dance," said Suzy, trying not to laugh. "You don't have to marry them!"

Bertie shuddered. He'd never danced with a girl in his life – except for the time Miss Boot forced him to try country dancing, and then he'd kept his eyes closed.

Dirty Bertie

"You've got to help me!" he begged.
"What can I do?"

Suzy folded her arms. "It's easy.
You've got two choices," she said.
"Either you miss the prom altogether …
or you find a girl to go with you."

Bertie buried his head in his hands.
It was too horrible! But if he missed the
prom, he'd be stuck in a room with Miss
Boot doing extra maths – a fate worse
than dancing!

CHAPTER 3

Friday, the dreaded day of the Prom Party, arrived. Bertie trailed down to breakfast.

"I'm feeling a bit sick," he croaked, pushing his cereal around his bowl.

"Nonsense, it's your Prom Party today," said Mum.

"I don't think I can go," moaned

Bertie. "I've got feet ache!"

Mum sighed. "Toothache, tummy ache, I've heard it all before, Bertie," she said. "You're going to school and that's the end of it."

Darren and Eugene were waiting for Bertie in the playground.

"Well?" asked Darren. "Have you found someone to take to the prom?"

Bertie shook his head.

"You better get a move on – it's this afternoon," said Eugene.

"Yes, we've asked our partners," boasted Darren.

"Seriously? WHO?" said Bertie.

Darren quickly looked around. Two girls were just entering the school gates.

"Them," said Darren.

"Pamela and Amanda?" said Bertie. "How did you manage it?"

"Oh, it was easy," shrugged Darren. "Wasn't it, Eugene?"

"Yes," agreed Eugene. "We just went straight up and asked them."

Bertie stared. Darren had never shown any interest in Pamela or Amanda before. And he couldn't remember Eugene ever actually speaking to a girl! All the same, if they both had prom partners he couldn't put it off any longer.

"What about Donna?" said Darren.

"Donna?" squeaked Bertie.

"Yes, I bet she'd go to the prom with you," said Eugene. "She likes you."

Bertie looked over at Donna, who was sitting on a wall waiting for her

friends. He didn't mind Donna – she was
clever and she knew a lot about dogs.
But as for asking her to the prom – he'd
rather ask a frog.

"Go on!" urged Darren. "While she's
by herself."

Bertie took a deep breath and
plodded over. His hands were sweating
and his throat was dry.

"Hi, Donna," he mumbled.

"Oh, hi, Bertie!" said Donna. "Okay?"

Dirty Bertie

"Yes ... fine, great, good," said Bertie. He hummed tunelessly and looked at the sky. His legs had started to tremble.

"Did you want something?" asked Donna.

"Me?"

"Yes, you looked like you wanted to say something," said Donna, frowning.

Just come straight out and ask her, thought Bertie. He cleared his throat.

"I was, um ... wondering ... if well..."

"Yes?" said Donna.

"If ... um ... you ... if you still have a dog?" stammered Bertie.

Dirty Bertie

"Cookie? Yes, I've still got him,"
replied Donna.

"Ah," said Bertie. "That's good. Well,
bye then!"

He fled back to his friends.

"Did you ask her?" asked Eugene.

"Yes," said Bertie. "She's still got
a dog."

The morning sped by without Bertie
having any success. Darren and Eugene
suggested four or five girls in their class
but Bertie's nerve failed him every time.
His mouth turned dry and his mind went
blank as soon as he got near them. Once
he tried passing a note to Kelly, which said:

> WILL YOO CUME TO THE PROM?

Dirty Bertie

But the note only reached Know-All Nick, who thought it was a joke and threw it back at Bertie. Time was running out. The prom was due to start at two o'clock – and Bertie still didn't have a partner.

"It's no use!" he sighed as he trailed outside at break. "I'll just have to go on my own."

"You can't" said Darren quickly. "They won't let you in."

"Won't they?"

"No, it's a prom!" said Darren. "They'll send you to Miss Boot."

"Anyway, you can't dance by yourself," argued Eugene.

Bertie didn't want to dance at all. He just wanted to sit watching a film like they always did.

DONK! Suddenly a
tennis ball hit him on the
head.

Bertie picked it up.
Angela Nicely came
running over. Angela
lived next door and
had been in love with
Bertie forever.

"Sorry, Bertie!" she
giggled. "Are you okay?"

A thought crept into Bertie's
head. Normally he avoided Angela like
a cold bath but this was an emergency.
He had to find someone to take to the
prom and she was his only chance. He
took a deep breath.

"Listen," he mumbled. "Do you, er …
want to go to this prom thing?"

Dirty Bertie

"I *am* going!" trilled Angela. "We're all going!"

"Yes, but I mean go with me," said Bertie, turning red.

Angela blinked. "With you? You mean go *together*?" she said.

Bertie gulped and nodded.

"Yee-hoo!" cried Angela. "Wait till I tell Laura and Maisie!"

She hugged him and ran off.

Bertie watched her go. What had he done? A Prom Party with adoring Angela sticking to him like glue. This was going to be the worst day of his life!

CHAPTER 4

At two o'clock, Bertie stood nervously outside the hall waiting for Angela. His suit itched and his bow tie was too tight. Inside he could hear loud music. The Prom Party was already in full swing.

Darren and Eugene arrived.

"So where is she?" asked Darren. "This mystery girlfriend of yours?"

"She's not my girlfriend," scowled Bertie. "It's just for the prom. Anyway, where are Pamela and Amanda?"

"Who?" said Eugene.

"Oh, they're meeting us inside," said Darren.

"Hi, Bertie!" squeaked an excited voice.

Darren and Eugene stared. Angela was wearing her frilly party dress with pink sparkly shoes and a new bow in her hair.

"Angela? *She's* your girlfriend?" hooted Darren.

"She's NOT my girlfriend!" groaned Bertie.

"You said!" pouted Angela. "You said you wanted to go together!"

"I do," said Bertie quickly. "But it's just for the prom, okay?"

Angela stuck out her bottom lip.

"Well if you're going to be mean…"
she said sulkily.

"Sorry," Bertie muttered. "Let's go in."

Angela brightened up and held out
her hand.

Bertie sighed and took it. This was
worse than the time he'd turned up for
swimming without his trunks.

"After you!" grinned Darren, holding
open the door.

Angela dragged him into the hall.

A song was just coming to an end.

"Here they are!" shouted Darren.
"Bertie and Angela!"

Everyone turned their way, staring in
boggle-eyed amazement.

Bertie couldn't believe it. The girls
were all in one corner while the boys
stood by the table eating crisps. No one

was dancing or holding hands, apart from
him. Darren and Eugene were giggling
like a pair of idiots. The horrible truth
dawned on Bertie. It was all a rotten
trick. No one else had brought a girl to
the prom.

"Your face! Hee hee!" hooted Darren.

"Ha ha! You actually fell for it!"
chuckled Eugene.

Dirty Bertie

Bertie dropped Angela's hand.

"Come on, Bertie, let's dance," she cried as the music started. "Oh, but what about your friends? They don't have anyone to dance with."

Bertie smiled. "Oh dear, that's no good," he said. "What shall we do?"

"I know," cried Angela. "Wait there! I'll get Maisie and Laura!"

Darren and Eugene looked horrified.

"No, no ... don't!" stammered Darren.

"We're fine," gulped Eugene.

But it was too late. Angela was already running over, towing her two friends behind her. Darren and Eugene backed away but Bertie made sure they didn't escape.

"Oh no," he said, "you can't come to

a Prom Party without a partner! And
anyway, I thought you *liked* dancing?"

CHAPTER 1

It was Wednesday afternoon and Gran had dropped in for tea, which always meant they had cake. Bertie reached out to grab the biggest slice.

"Bertie!" groaned Mum. "Guests first, please!"

"Have shum cake, Gran," said Bertie with his mouth full.

Dirty Bertie

"Sorry, Gran," sighed Mum. "What were you saying?"

"This Saturday," said Gran, "it's the Sunset Club's annual coach trip. We're going to Skegby-on-Sea."

"That'll be nice," said Mum.

"Yes," said Gran. "A few people have dropped out, so I did wonder if Bertie might like to come?"

"ME? WHERE?" asked Bertie, spraying cake crumbs everywhere.

Gran dusted off the front of her dress with a tissue.

"On a day trip to Skegby," she said.

"It's at the seaside," added Mum.

Dirty Bertie

The seaside? Bertie's eyes lit up. He hadn't been to the seaside in years – at least since last summer. Hang on, though, he'd learned to be careful when Gran was handing out invitations. The last time she offered to take him to the cinema her new boyfriend, Reg, had come along. Bertie had been forced to spill his Strawberry Slushy in Reg's lap to stop them kissing!

Dirty Bertie

"Who's going?" he asked suspiciously.

"I told you – my friends from the Sunset Club," replied Gran. "You remember Sherry?"

Bertie could hardly forget her – when Sherry and Gran got together they were like a pair of naughty schoolgirls. Sherry wore bright red lipstick and giggled a lot.

"Is everyone going to be *old*?" asked Bertie.

"No, mostly my age," answered Gran.

Dirty Bertie

"You mean a hundred?" said Bertie.

"*Sixty-seven*, if you don't mind," huffed Gran. "But don't let me force you, Bertie, I just thought it would be a treat."

"It sounds fun," said Mum, seeing the chance of a Bertie-free day. "You could build sandcastles on the beach, maybe even paddle in the sea."

Bertie considered it. "Are any other children going?" he asked.

"I doubt it," said Gran, "but it's always a great day out. Our tour guide Gerry's a scream. We play bingo and crazy golf and sing songs all the way home."

Bertie frowned. He'd heard Gran's singing and she sounded like she was in pain. Imagine fifty or more grannies warbling away on a coach! He'd have to take earplugs. All the same, it *was* a trip to the seaside and the best part was that Gran always paid for everything.

"Of course it's up to you," said Mum, pouring more tea. "But I'm pretty sure Skegby has a funfair."

"A FUNFAIR!" cried Bertie.

That settled it, he was definitely going.

CHAPTER 2

On Saturday morning Dad dropped them in town at the coach pick-up point. Bertie had brought everything he needed for the day – swimming trunks, towel, rubber ring, bucket and spade, plus enough sweets to last a month.

"Are you sure you're going to need all that?" Gran asked.

233

"I always bring this stuff to the seaside," replied Bertie.

He looked around at the crowd waiting to board the coach. Everyone seemed to be ancient.

"They're even older than you, Gran," he said.

"SHH! Not so loud!" hissed Gran.

Sherry spotted them and came bustling over.

"Hello, Dotty," she cooed. "And I've met this handsome young man before. Are you sitting next to me, Bertie? Hee hee!"

Bertie shrank back as Sherry planted a big sloppy kiss on his cheek. He hoped it wasn't going to be like this all day. If everyone wanted to kiss him, he'd have to wear a bucket over his head.

"Right, are we all here?" asked a loud voice.

A tall, prim woman holding a clipboard stood at the coach door. She had a beaky nose and a stern expression.

"Who's that?" asked Gran. "Where's Gerry?"

"Oh, didn't you hear? He's poorly," sighed Sherry. "They've sent us this one, instead – her name's Miss Stickler."

Dirty Bertie

Gran stared in dismay. "But Gerry always takes us to Skegby," she said. "He's the reason it's so much fun!"

Bertie didn't think Miss Stickler looked like she'd heard of fun. She was making everyone form an orderly line as if they were back at school.

"Goodness – who's this?" she asked, when she saw Bertie.

"This is my grandson Bertie," explained Gran.

"Isn't he a bit young for the Sunset Club?" said Miss Stickler. "I hope he's going to behave himself."

Dirty Bertie

"Of course he is," said Gran. "Bertie's never any trouble, are you, Bertie?"

"No," said Bertie, which was partly true. He never *meant* to be any trouble, it was just that trouble had a habit of following him around.

The coach set off. To Bertie's relief, Gran sat down beside him while Sherry took a seat with a chap called Ted. Once they were on the motorway, Miss Stickler stood up.

"Good morning and welcome," she said. "As you may know, Gerry has lost his voice and sadly can't be with us. But the good news is – I'm going to be your tour guide for the day. I have drawn up a timetable of activities and I'm sure we'll all have a wonderful day. Are there any questions?"

Bertie raised his hand. "When do we go to the funfair?" he asked.

Miss Stickler pulled a face. "I hardly think anyone wants to visit the *funfair*," she sniffed. "In any case, it's not on my timetable."

Bertie blinked. *Not go to the funfair?* But that was the whole point of coming!

Gran patted his hand. "Don't worry, Bertie," she whispered. "I'm sure we can pop along there at some point."

CHAPTER 3

At last the coach arrived at Skegby-on-Sea. Bertie and Gran waited to get off. It had been a long journey with about a hundred stops for the toilet. Miss Stickler had spent the whole time telling Bertie off – for kicking the seat in front, dropping sweet wrappers and making rude noises with his rubber ring.

239

Dirty Bertie

As they got out, Miss Stickler handed everyone a printed sheet.

"What's this?" asked Gran.

"Our timetable for today," replied Miss Stickler. "There's one each so that everyone's clear what we're doing and at what time."

Bertie read down the list. There were visits to tea shops, an antiques market, a church and the Skegby Pencil Museum. There was no mention of paddling, sandcastles or going anywhere near the funfair.

"It's the seaside!" Bertie grumbled. "We have to go to the beach."

"It's far too windy," said Miss Stickler. "I don't want anyone catching a cold."

"We could play football," suggested Bertie. "That would warm us up!"

Dirty Bertie

"This is a trip for the elderly," sniffed Miss Stickler. "I think you'll find my programme has something for everyone."

"Not for me," muttered Gran. "Where's the bingo?"

"And the crazy golf?" added Sherry.

"Gerry always takes us to the pier," grumbled Ted loudly.

Dirty Bertie

"Well, Gerry isn't here," snapped Miss Stickler. "I think you'll find the Pencil Museum is really quite exciting. Now follow me, please, and try to keep up."

She set off, marching down the road with her umbrella held high.

Gran shook her head. "You can go off people," she muttered.

Dirty Bertie

"I didn't like her from the start," said
Sherry.

Bertie trailed along with Gran, wearing
his rubber ring and dragging his bucket
and spade. He stared longingly at the
beach, where a few children were
playing on the sand.

"Can't I stay here?" he moaned.

Dirty Bertie

"Sorry, Bertie," sighed Gran. "I promised your mum I wouldn't let you out of my sight. Maybe we'll have time for the beach or the funfair later?"

But Miss Stickler had other ideas. She marched them from one boring place to the next. The Pencil Museum had a thrilling display of 300 pencils, while the antiques market had endless stalls selling piles of old junk. As they walked along the seafront, Bertie could see the bright lights of the funfair and hear the occasional snatch of music. It was torture being so close.

"Mum promised me the funfair!" he grumbled.

"Believe me, I'd love to go," sighed Gran. "But it's not on the blooming timetable."

Dirty Bertie

Later that afternoon they made their second tea stop. Bertie looked around the café gloomily. Ted seemed to have nodded off while the rest of the party looked dead on their feet. The coach was due to leave at five, which meant they had less than two hours.

"Can't we go to the funfair *now*?" Bertie begged Gran.

Gran sighed. "I'm sorry, Bertie, I've told you – I'm not in charge."

"Pity," sighed Sherry. "I do love a good funfair!"

Ted suddenly sat up and opened his eyes. "A funfair? I haven't been to one of those in years!" he cried.

Bertie glanced over at Miss Stickler, who was nibbling a teacake. If she wouldn't take them then they'd just have to find another way.

"Why don't we escape?" he whispered.

"ESCAPE?" asked Gran.

"Yes," said Bertie. "If we can give her the slip, what's to stop us? We can all go."

Gran and Sherry looked at each other.

"How exciting!" giggled Sherry. "It'll be like one of those films where they break out of prison."

"Do we have to dig a tunnel?" asked
Ted.

Bertie shook his head. "No. We just
need old Sticklepants out of the way for
five minutes."

He explained his plan while the other
three listened, nodding their heads. The
Great Escape was on, but they'd have to
move fast. Smuggling fifty pensioners out
of a teashop right under Miss Stickler's
nose wasn't going to be easy!

CHAPTER 4

"Oh dear! Oh no! Where can it be?" wailed Gran, her head in her hands.

Bertie thought that she was overacting but it did the trick – Miss Stickler was coming over.

"What's the matter?" she demanded.

"I can't find my purse," said Gran.

"Well, where did you last have it?"

asked Miss Stickler.

"Um, let me think … in the toilets … yes, that was it," said Gran.

Miss Stickler sighed. Old people were always losing things. If it wasn't money, it was their keys or their false teeth.

Gran led the way to the ladies' toilets and opened the door.

"After you," she said politely.

Miss Stickler went in. There was no sign of the purse by the basins. She opened a cubicle door and looked on the floor.

"Are you sure you——?"

WHAM!

Suddenly the door to the ladies' toilets slammed shut. Miss Stickler stared round in surprise.

"HEY! WHAT'S GOING ON?" she

cried, trying the door handle. It refused
to open.

Outside, Bertie helped Gran to wedge
the door shut with a chair.

"Quick!" said Bertie. "Let's go before
she gets out!"

Dirty Bertie

Gran and Sherry rounded up the rest of the party, which wasn't easy. Some of them protested they hadn't finished their tea.

"Sorry, there isn't time," said Gran, glancing at the toilets. "Please do hurry!"

THUMP! THUMP!

"LET ME OUT!" yelled Miss Stickler, banging on the door.

"Come *on!*" urged Bertie, herding the group out of the café. "Head for the funfair. It's time we enjoyed ourselves!"

"The bus fare?" said one lady. "I thought we came by coach!"

THUD! THUD! CRASH!

The door to the ladies' toilets finally burst open and Miss Stickler stumbled

out. She was astonished to find the café
deserted. Toasted teacakes sat on plates
half eaten, with the tea still warm in the
cups.

A waitress appeared
holding a tray.

"Where did they all go?"
demanded Miss Stickler.
"The old people!"

"I've no idea," replied the
waitress. "They
just got up and
left all of a sudden.
But someone will
have to pay the bill."
Miss Stickler glared and
fished out her purse. She had
a pretty good idea who was
behind this.

Dirty Bertie

"Wheee! Hold tight, Bertie!" squealed Gran.

Bertie hung on as the big wheel took them round again. The funfair had proved a big hit with the Sunset Club. Many of them said they hadn't had such a great time in years. They'd whooped on the dodgems, screamed on the ghost train and had to sit down after getting dizzy on the merry-go-round.

"That was a hoot!" giggled Sherry, as the big wheel came to a stop. "What shall we do next?"

Dirty Bertie

Bertie lifted the safety barrier and climbed out. His face fell. A tall, stern woman was marching towards them.

"STOP RIGHT THERE!" shouted Miss Stickler. "I knew you were behind all this."

Bertie gulped. Miss Stickler's face was bright red. She looked like she'd run a marathon.

"How *dare* you?" she stormed. "Locking me in the toilets. I've had to chase all over town looking for you!"

Dirty Bertie

"Oh dear!" said Gran. "You poor thing. You'd better sit down."

Gran nudged Bertie, who took a moment to catch on.

"Yes, have a seat," said Bertie, taking Miss Stickler's arm.

He helped her into a padded seat, framed by coloured lights.

"You should be ashamed," Miss Stickler panted. "Behaving like schoolkids."

"I am a schoolkid," replied Bertie. "Now hold on tight."

"What?" asked Miss Stickler, confused.

CLUNK!

The safety barrier came down over her head and music began to play.

Miss Stickler looked around in panic. Her seat was slowly rising off the ground. She was on the big wheel and it was taking her up!

"HEEEELP!" she squawked. "GET ME DOWN!"

"Bye, bye, Miss Stickler!" cried Bertie, waving from below.

"Well, that ought to keep her busy for a while," smiled Gran. "So what's next then, Bertie?"

"The helter skelter!" cried Bertie. "Come on, I'll race you!"

CHAPTER 1

Bertie had seen the worm farm in a shop window when he was passing with his mum. He could hardly believe his eyes. Who needed sheep and cows when you could own a farm with real live worms? He'd decided there and then he had to have it.

Bertie loved worms and they made

the perfect pets. He still hadn't forgotten Arthur, his pet worm who'd lived in his bedroom until Mum discovered him. But a worm farm was even better – you got a whole family of worms for just £9.99!

The only problem was, Bertie didn't have £9.99. He'd spent all his pocket money on sweets and it was no good asking his family to help. Dad said worms belonged in the garden, Mum thought they were revolting, while Gran screamed if she came near one.

On the way to school, Bertie asked his friends to help.

"Ten pounds? For a bunch of worms?" said Darren. "You must be joking!"

"It's a worm farm," explained Bertie. "You can watch them squirming about."

Dirty Bertie

"Yuck!" said Darren. "Anyway, I haven't got ten pounds."

Bertie sighed. "What about you, Eugene?"

"I'm not that keen on worms," said Eugene.

"Yes, but can you lend me ten pounds?" said Bertie.

Eugene shook his head. "Sorry, Bertie, I'm saving up for a new violin case."

Dirty Bertie

Bertie rolled his eyes. So much for friends! Didn't they know how important this was? It might be his one and only chance to own a worm farm!

There had to be someone who would lend him ten pounds. It was no use asking Know-All Nick – he wouldn't lend Bertie a used hanky. But what about Royston Rich? He had pots of money! He was always boasting that his dad was practically a millionaire.

There was just one snag – Royston and Bertie weren't friends. Royston had never forgiven him for ruining his swimming party when Whiffer left a present in his pool.

Still, it was worth a try – Royston was probably the one person in his class who actually HAD ten pounds.

Dirty Bertie

At school Bertie tracked down
Royston in the playground.

"Hi, Royston, old pal," said Bertie.

"What do *you* want?" Royston
scowled.

"Nothing," said Bertie. "Only, I was
just wondering – how much pocket
money do you get a week?"

"Loads more than you," boasted
Royston.

"Great," said Bertie. "In that case,
could you lend me ten pounds?"

Dirty Bertie

"TEN POUNDS?" cried Royston.

"Yes, to buy a worm farm," explained Bertie. "I'll pay you back."

"No chance!" snorted Royston. "I wouldn't lend you ten pounds if you got down on your knees and begged!" A sly look crossed his face. "But if you REALLY want the money…" he said.

"I'll do anything," said Bertie.

Dirty Bertie

"Okay then, what if I pay you ten pounds – to be my slave for the day?" said Royston.

Bertie gulped. "W-what?"

"You heard me," said Royston. He pulled out a ten pound note from his pocket and waved it in the air.

"Uh-uh," he said, as Bertie reached out. "You have to earn it first. Do we have a deal?"

Bertie thought fast. He couldn't imagine anything worse than being Royston's slave. He'd rather marry Angela Nicely! On the other hand, it'd take him years to save up enough pocket money to buy the worm farm himself.

"Okay, it's a deal," he said.

Royston gave a goofy grin as he shook Bertie's hand.

Dirty Bertie

"Super!" he said. "Of course my slave has to do anything I want — all day."

"Just until the end of school," said Bertie.

"Let's say four o'clock," said Royston.

He rubbed his hands with glee. He'd always wanted his own slave. Bertie had no idea what he'd let himself in for!

CHAPTER 2

"What was all that about?" asked Eugene when Bertie returned.

"I've just agreed to be Royston's slave," said Bertie.

"Are you MAD?" asked Darren.

Bertie shrugged. "He's paying me ten pounds."

"Yes, but you have to be his slave!"

Dirty Bertie

"Only for today," said Bertie.

"You wouldn't catch me being Royston's slave!" said Darren. "You know what he's like."

Bertie knew only too well. Royston was born ordering people around. He probably had servants at home to fold his clothes, do his homework and brush his teeth.

"It can't be that bad," said Bertie.

"I wouldn't bet on it," said Eugene. "He'll probably treat you like dirt."

"OH SLAVE!" sang a voice. "Where has my slave got to?"

Darren raised his eyebrows. "Better not keep his lordship waiting," he said.

Bertie trailed over.

"Where were you?" demanded Royston.

Dirty Bertie

"With my friends," answered Bertie.

"I didn't give you time off," said Royston. "And call me 'master' or 'your highness'."

Bertie frowned. He could think of a lot of other things to call Royston.

"What do you want then, *master*?" he asked.

"And bow when you're speaking to me," said Royston.

Bertie glared. This was pushing things too far. He ducked his head, hoping that no one was watching.

"My shoes are dirty," said Royston.

"They look fine to me," said Bertie.

"If I say they're dirty, then they're dirty," said Royston. And to prove his point, he stepped in a big muddy puddle.

"Clean them, slave," he ordered.

Bertie gaped. "What with?"

"That's your problem," said Royston. "When I give you an order, I expect you to do it – and I told you to call me master."

Bertie was about to tell Royston to clean his own stupid shoes – but slaves weren't allowed to answer back. He kneeled down and wiped Royston's shoes with a grubby tissue.

"There, all done," he said.

Royston folded his arms. "I want them polished, slave," he said. "I want to see my face in them."

Bertie got back on his knees. Luckily, just at that moment, the bell rang. For once Bertie couldn't wait to go into school. At least Royston wouldn't be able to order him around in class.

CHAPTER 3

"Hurry up and sit down!" barked Miss Boot.

Bertie went to take his usual seat with his friends.

"Not there, slave!" said Royston. "You're sitting next to me."

"But that's my seat, I always sit there," protested Bertie.

"Not today," said Royston. "You sit where you're told."

"BERTIE!" thundered Miss Boot. "Why are you still wandering around? Find a seat!"

Bertie slumped into the chair beside Royston. He'd been hoping to get away from him in lessons. Still, he just had to stick it out until four o'clock, then he'd have ten whole pounds to spend.

Miss Boot went round, handing out worksheets.

"We'll begin with a maths test," she said. "You have thirty minutes to finish. And I expect you all to work in total silence."

Bertie groaned. He hated maths tests – the questions made his brain hurt. They were always about Peter, Susan and Nadia, who had eight sweets and added four and then took away three. Why couldn't they just get on and eat them?

"Slave!" Royston hissed in his ear.

Bertie groaned. "What now?"

"What now, *master*?" Royston insisted.

"I'm trying to work!" said Bertie.

Royston slid his test paper across the desk.

"You can do mine," he said. "I'm too tired to think about maths today."

"WHAT? I can't!" argued Bertie.

"Of course you can, that's what slaves are for," said Royston.

Bertie glanced up at Miss Boot, who had her eye on the class.

"We'll get caught!" he whispered.

"Then I'll say *you* were copying *me*,"

said Royston. "Hurry up – and make
sure you get a better mark than last
time."

Royston sat back in his seat. Bertie
couldn't believe it! How was he meant
to do Royston's test as well as his own?
He had a good mind to chuck Royston's
paper in the bin. But that would put an
end to their deal. He'd just have to work
at double speed.

Dirty Bertie

As the clock ticked, Bertie scribbled answers on Royston's test paper, writing down the first thing that came into his head. If Royston came bottom of the class, that was his own fault, he thought. Finally he completed the last question – now to start on his own paper…

"Right, everyone put down your pens!" boomed Miss Boot. "Who has completed all the questions?"

A few hands went up – one of them was Royston's.

"I have, Miss Boot!" he smirked.

"Excellent, Royston, and what about you, Bertie?" asked Miss Boot.

"Um, I made a start…" mumbled Bertie.

"Let me see," said Miss Boot marching over.

"All you've written is your name!" she snapped. "Idling as usual! You can have extra maths homework tonight."

Bertie glared at Royston, who wagged his finger and tutted.

"Oh dear, Bertie!" he jeered. "You never learn, do you?"

CHAPTER 4

Bertie slaved for Royston all morning.
At lunch Royston wanted his slave to
wait on him at the table. Bertie was
kept running back and forth to fetch
salt, ketchup, napkins and a clean spoon.
When he finally sat down to eat, his
food had gone stone cold.

During the afternoon it poured with

rain. Royston demanded to be sheltered under an umbrella while Bertie got soaked to the skin. By home time, Bertie was cold, wet, and sick and tired of being a slave. Still he'd done it – he'd made it to the end of the day and the reward was his!

"Ten pounds," he said to Royston in the cloakroom. "You owe me."

Royston checked his watch. "Actually the deal was until four o'clock," he reminded Bertie. "Which means we still have a good half an hour of slaving left."

He dumped his school bag at Bertie's feet.

"Carry that home, slave," he said. "And don't drop it."

Dirty Bertie

Bertie counted to ten. He wanted to throw the bag at Royston's big head. But he was so close to getting his hands on the money, he couldn't give up now.

"You coming, Bertie?" asked Darren.

Bertie sighed. "Royston wants me to carry his bag home," he said.

"Tell him to carry his own bag!" said Eugene.

"I can't, not until four o'clock!"

Darren and Eugene shook their heads. They couldn't believe Bertie was putting up with this!

They walked home together, taking the long way via Royston's house. Bertie had to lug Royston's bag as well as his own.

"It's so useful having a slave," Royston told Darren. "You really should try it some time."

Dirty Bertie

They stopped. They'd just turned into
the alleyway that led to Royston's road
but a giant puddle blocked the way. It
was about a dozen paces across and
looked at least ankle deep.

"We'll have to go round the other
way," said Eugene.

"I don't think so," said Royston,
glancing at his watch. "It'll take ages.
We can get across."

Dirty Bertie

"How?" asked Bertie.

"Simple. You'll just have to carry me," replied Royston.

Bertie stared at him. "You are kidding?" he said.

"Like I told you, that's what slaves are for," said Royston smugly. "I'm not getting my shoes wet."

"You're not really going to carry him?" said Darren.

"Tell him to get lost," advised Eugene.

Bertie looked at the wide brown puddle, then at Royston waiting to be carried across like royalty. All day he'd had to put up with that goofy face grinning at him. Well, no more, thought Bertie. There was only so much a person could take – even for a worm farm.

Royston climbed on to his back.

"Comfortable, your lordship?" said
Bertie.

"Yes, and don't forget my bag," said
Royston. "Come on, slave, giddy up!"

Bertie waded into the brown puddle,
with Royston's bag in one hand. The
water was so deep it sloshed over his
shoes and soaked his socks. Halfway
across he suddenly came to a halt.

"I didn't say stop!" shrieked Royston.
"KEEP GOING!"

Dirty Bertie

Bertie shook his head. "Ten pounds," he said. "By your watch, time's up, so hand it over."

"MOVE, SLAVE!" ordered Royston, digging his heels into Bertie's ribs.

Bertie didn't budge. "It's your last chance," he warned Royston.

"Don't answer back, and call me master!" shouted Royston, whacking Bertie on the shoulder.

That did it. Bertie let go of Royston's legs.

"ARGHHH! I'M ALL WET!" Royston howled, landing on his back. "HELP ME UP, YOU STUPID SLAVE!"

Royston raised a hand, which Bertie ignored. He dropped Royston's bag in the puddle with a splash.

"UGH! YOU… YOU…" cried Royston.

Bertie left Royston kicking his legs like a beetle on its back and returned to his friends.

"I think you can say goodbye to that ten pounds," said Eugene.

Bertie shrugged. "I know … but I've waited all day to do that and it was worth every penny!"

Royston scrambled to his feet and squelched to the other side of the puddle.

He turned back, waved his fists and yelled, "I HATE YOU!"

Bertie bowed low. "And the same to you, your highness," he said.

Look out for:

DAVID ROBERTS WRITTEN BY ALAN MACDONALD

Dirty Bertie

TROUBLE!